THICKNESS
OF
BLOOD

By Kimberly Gould

Martin Sisters Publishing

Published by

Ivy House Books, a division of Martin Sisters Publishing, LLC

www. martinsisterspublishing. com

Copyright © 2012 Kimberly Gould

ISBN: 978-1-937273-62-0
Fiction
Cover design by Wendy Blubaugh
Printed in the United States of America
Martin Sisters Publishing, LLC

DEDICATION

To Richard and Deborah, I'm bound to you by more than blood.

ACKNOWLEGEMENTS

Many people read Thickness of Blood in its various stages. I'd like to thank Denise Melton for her early stage advice, which lead to my first major rewrite. Angela Matson, Deadra Krieger, Miranda Gammella, and David Kirk for not only reading and advising, but supporting and encouraging me when I felt down and out with the whole process. Thanks to Eileen Cook for her advice on where to start the first chapter. Jeanne Henderson helped on the final drafts. Kathleen Papajohn deserves recognition for the polish she gave this piece at the very end. Thank you, all, for your criticism, your encouragement, your praise. Thanks also to Melissa Newman for her work on the cover and all the other behind the scenes publishing she did with her sister Denise.

An imprint of Martin Sisters Publishing, LLC

Chapter One

George stepped wearily into the entrance of his home. The smell of beef stew had been evident through the door, making his mouth water. The clinking of dishes reached him as his family, hearing his truck pull into the drive, was setting supper on the table. Poking his head around the doorjamb, he saw two brown-haired girls all but racing each other around the table. They smiled and giggled, each egging the other on.

"Slow down!" Eva cried. "You'll break something."

The girls stopped abruptly, dropping cutlery in a clatter on the Formica table.

"I didn't mean you were finished!" Eva argued as they tore off into another room. "Janet! Marlene! You get back here!" The adolescent girls pretended not to hear, the television drowning their mother out.

Eva sighed before turning to George who bent slightly to kiss her lips. With none of the girls around, he slipped an arm around her still small waist, hand on her ample hip.

"George," she scolded. "Your hands are dirty." Her blue eyes were menacing, but lightened quickly. "If they were clean ..." She let the implication hang in the air to tempt him.

With a grin, he strode past her to the bathroom, passing his third daughter on the way. "Daphne," he said simply, nodding to her.

"Dad. You look tired. Can I get you a drink?" A small crease disappeared from her forehead as she smiled.

"You look a little tired yourself, sweetheart. School harder this year than last?" he asked.

"Not so much," she said.

"Good," he said, closing the door to the bathroom and unfastening his fly. He wondered what it was if not school? Probably boys, he thought, scowling at the contents of the cabinet over the toilet. He was going to be beating them off soon. Zipping up, he wondered that he hadn't already. Daphne was sixteen, after all, and pretty. Were the boys slow, or was she beating them away herself, he wondered as he washed his hands.

Taking a cloth from the cabinet, he pulled off his shirt and washed first his face and neck, then under his arms, planning to shower later, after sitting down with his family.

He took the seat at the head of the table as Eva scooped out a ladle of the stew and set it before him. He looked up at his wife, then over at each of his daughters, meeting brown and hazel eyes around the table.

"Tell me," he said, looking first at Janet, "what you learned today in school."

It was his favorite way to start a meal. He felt so far from his daughters, especially when jobs like his last came. He'd been out of town for a month at a time over the summer, erecting an office building in Pueblo. Hotels and restaurant food paled next to his wife's cooking and bed.

He listened to his daughters tell of their day at school, Janet and Marlene talking over one another some of the time. George noticed that the oldest two women, daughter and wife, were also the most quiet.

"Eva? Anything interesting today?"

His wife sighed and told of a trip to the market, a call from her mother that went on far too long, and promised the rest of her day was even less interesting. Smiling to his wife, George turned his gaze to his oldest daughter.

"Daphne? Anything interesting happen to you today?"

She shifted a little in her chair, pushing her peas around her bowl in the remaining gravy, not answering at first. Both the other girls had had second helpings of stew, but Daphne, who usually ate as much, wasn't finished with her first helping. "Nothing, a test in English. I think I did alright." She didn't quite meet his eyes, but smiled.

George smiled back, stretching. "I'm sure you did. Well, ladies, that was an excellent meal, thank you." He sat back a little in his chair. "If you don't mind, I'll retire to the lounge," he said loftily with a smirk. The family room was hardly a lounge, but his recliner lounged, so it seemed appropriate to him.

Eva chuckled, kissing his cheek. "I'll bring you a drink," she offered.

"No need." As he stretched, he felt the dirt still under his shirt and pants. "I'm going to shower first anyway. I'll grab it myself on the way. You do ... whatever it is you do when I'm not here," he teased, touching her hip lightly.

She giggled and he felt his heart jump a little. She hadn't giggled like that since they were dating. A month was simply too long away. He would have to take jobs in town from now on. George left the kitchen as the younger girls cleared the table and Daphne filled the sink with water. It was still running when he closed the door to the bathroom.

He undressed slowly, even though he was already a garment short, giving the sink in the kitchen time to fill. He wouldn't linger; a sink full wasn't much, but the hot water tank wasn't huge either. He let the water beat out a knot in his upper back before washing the dust out of his hair.

Towelling off, he wrapped the terrycloth around his hips before walking to the bedroom.

"Daddy's naked!" one of the younger girls, Janet he thought, shouted. She was only twelve and still got a kick out of such things.

"Shhh!" Marlene hissed.

George saw neither and closed the door behind him, changing into flannel pants and a robe. He pulled on slippers and stepped back out. He found Daphne still in the kitchen with a whiskey and Pepsi on the counter for him, courtesy of Eva. Picking up his drink, he watched his eldest putting away the dishes.

She stretched to put up the bowls, her ponytail hanging toward her left hip. She put away a pot and leaned on the left again, tipping in that direction. George sipped his drink, trying to remember if he'd noticed her favoring her left side before. She turned to face him, taking a quick step on her right leg before leaning again on the left.

"Dad," she said, surprised. "I didn't hear you. Mom made your drink." She looked at it in his hand.

He nodded. "I found it. What did you do to your leg?" he asked. "You didn't mention it at supper."

"Nothing. I ... fell. Embarrassing and uninteresting." Daphne's voice was soft, timid.

"You're sure it isn't bothering you?" he asked, reaching out to put a hand on her shoulder.

She shook her head and smiled, rolling down the sleeves of her rose cardigan. "No, it's fine. Just a bad bruise. Embarrassing, like I said." She didn't meet his eyes at first, but finally, when his hand stayed heavy on her arm, looked up, her brown eyes shining.

Her smile seemed sure enough, so he patted her shoulder before pulling her into a hug and kissing the top of her head. "I love you, little bug," he whispered.

"Da-ad," she complained, hating the baby name.

He chuckled and let her go. "Well, I missed you. Seems you were 'little bug' not that long ago."

"You weren't gone that long."

He nodded, taking his drink into the lounge. He watched his wife stitching something onto one of the girls' skirts. The younger two watched the television. He tried to follow the Rockford Files, but his eyes kept drifting shut.

He was woken by a kiss on his cheek and a weight in his lap.

"The girls are in bed," Eva murmured, her lips finding his in the dark.

His hands fondled the familiar curves of his wife. They hadn't been apart so long that he could forget those. His hand held hip, breast and cheek. He brushed a thigh, stroking up and finding nothing beneath.

He groaned slightly, feeling a stirring in his groin at the knowledge. "Ev." He kissed her again, tenderly, moving his hand to her face, holding both cheeks.

She seemed to melt against him. Her body, so soft and rounded, fit perfectly to his. One of her hands slid down his chest, opening his robe and reaching his soft pants that were already tenting. Her touch made him leap to her, standing erect.

She chuckled quietly. "Always so obedient," she teased, touching him through the cotton. "He knows just what I want."

George fought a growl, agreeing with his baser nature on what they wanted. His hand passed down his wife's back to pull up the skirt of her gown and hold her bottom, thick callused fingers feeling her soft skin. Her breath staggered as he pulled her closer, pressed his fingers further, touching where she was hottest.

"Should we take this to the bedroom?" he asked, breathless.

She wrenched down his pants enough to free him. "Why wait?" she asked, sliding over him.

George's head fell back. He wasn't even inside her yet, and he was throbbing. "Slow," he groaned, almost begging.

Her eyes sparkled even in the dark, catching the streetlight as she weighed his request. "No." She moved her hips against his, rubbing herself along him. George closed his eyes, his belly tightening.

"Jeee-sus, Eva. I would have whacked if I'd known." His apology went unheard as Eva reached around, spreading herself.

Biting his lip to try to hold on, he lifted her up, his tip burning against her. "Shiiiiit," he groaned, making a mess of her gown. Eva continued to ride, palming her chest as she clenched her jaw and made small sounds of her own.

She slowed and panted, her closed eyes opening on his. He could see her outline clearly by the streetlight streaming through the window. She was beautiful, her hair free down her back, over her shoulders.

Her breath wasn't quite as heavy as his. "We could go to the bedroom now," she suggested. Her teeth shone for a moment as she grinned.

With a growl into her neck, George scooped her up, collapsing the recliner and carrying her to bed. He thought he heard something from Daphne's room, but it sounded like a snore. He shook it from his mind, easily replaced with plans to pleasure his wife.

Saturday, George was headed home from work. They were pushing to get walls of the Manson house up, working six days instead of seven. Saturday was only a half-day, trying to find some time for life and family. He noticed a boy standing on the porch, one George didn't recognize.

"Hello," he said, wiping his hand on his work pants before extending it. "I'm George."

"Uh ... Adam." The boy seemed startled but took George's hand in his own. It was covered in scratches and he had stitches over his eye.

"I'm ready," Daphne said, stepping out of the door, pulling a light sweater over her maxi dress.

George's eye immediately went to the brown and green bruises that covered her upper arms, the darkest point on her biceps.

He looked from her to Adam. "You had best tell me you didn't give her those," he growled, looking through the boy's glasses into his wide brown eyes.

"No! Dad, no!" Daphne shook her head, jumping down a stair to take her father's arms in her hands. "No," she said softly, turning him to look at her. "It wasn't Adam. He got hurt trying to protect me."

George took a breath. That made sense. He wouldn't be meeting Daphne today if he'd hurt her a few days ago. If that were the case, who had given Daphne those bruises?

"What happened?" George demanded.

Daphne looked to Adam who nodded to her. George ground his teeth. Why did she need his permission?

"It was ... James. James Spencer." If it hadn't been so quiet on the street, George would never have made out the name.

George took a moment but couldn't recall ever hearing about James. As he thought, he remembered hearing Adam's name before, a boy at school, a new friend.

"Does your mother know?"

"No!" Daphne said sharply, looking up. "No one knows." She let go of her father and held her own arms curling in on herself, her small frame shaking.

Adam came behind her and put his hands over hers whispering in her ear. George nearly tore the boy's hands away, but whatever he said to Daphne had worked. She lifted her head, tears streaking her cheeks.

She sniffed. "James ... it's been ... It started two years ago, Dad."

George wobbled where he stood. Two years? He hadn't been gone two years, only two months, closer to three, but still. He reached out to grip the rail of the stairs for support.

"T-two years?" he asked, his voice low and harsh. "And you never ..." He shook his head. The town was small. Surely a secret this big couldn't be kept. And if it could, they'd raised Daphne better than that. If he was someone close to her, she would have mentioned him at the very least.

Still, the only boy he could remember being mentioned was Adam. "You've been friends over the summer?" he asked the boy.

Adam's smile was slightly rueful. "Yes, sir. A little more than friends." He put his hands on Daphne's shoulders. "I was hoping she'd introduce me soon."

Daphne continued to shake and started to cry. "I ... I can't." She tore from Adam, running up the stairs, into the house.

Eva came out onto the porch. "What's happened to her? Oh, hello, Adam."

George's jaw ached from clenching, but it tightened further when his wife smiled familiarly at the boy he'd just met. George worked to ease the stiffness. "You've met?" he asked.

"Just once. A couple weeks ago he came to help Daphne with some homework. Math wasn't it?"

"Trig, ma'am," Adam said, tipping his head a little to George's wife.

"George? Is something the matter?" Eva asked, concern on her face. George eased a little more at Adam's deference and manners but was still grimacing at the thought of his daughter hiding a boy from him.

"I think he wasn't quite ready to meet me, Mrs. Kingston. It was a bit of a shock."

George lifted his eyes enough to meet Adam's. The statement was true enough but avoided what was really bothering George. It also reminded him that Eva knew nothing about James either. "Yes," he told his wife, "just caught by surprise."

"Well, George, surely Daphne is old enough to have boys who are friends."

George's gaze whipped up to his wife, brows raised. "You didn't know either?"

"Um, what he's saying is ... I mean, ma'am," Adam stumbled to explain.

"What I mean is that he's more than a friend," George said, his jaw clenching again. He should be ready to let his daughter date at sixteen, especially with someone she brought to the house to meet them, someone who was willing to step in the way to help her, but he wasn't. Daphne was his little girl and he wasn't ready to share her with any boy.

"Really?!" Eva sounded surprised and pleased. "Well, that's good news. Will you join us for dinner tonight, Adam?"

"Uh ..." he looked to George who gave a slight shake of the head. George did *not* want to try to eat with this young man at the table. "I'll need to talk with my mother. She's expecting me."

"Of course, you can use our phone," Eva said, gesturing for Adam to follow her.

"I think I'll talk to him a bit, Eva." George interrupted.

Eva looked at her husband, probably wondering why he wasn't as happy as she was. Smoothing her apron, she turned back to the house. "Very well. I do hope you will stay," she said over her shoulder before closing the door.

George sighed and sat on a step, putting his head in his hands. The world was spinning out of his control. He'd thought about Daphne and boys, but thinking about it and having the boy in front of him were two different things. And that was before considering those bruises.

"Tell me about James," George demanded.

Adam sat on the step beside him. "He graduated in June. I thought it was over. I..."

George glared at the boy during his pause. "That doesn't tell me anything."

"Right, sorry. The beginning. I noticed Daphne in April. She had a bruise on her cheek, one she said came from a fall." Adam looked at George for confirmation of the event. George remembered what Daphne had told him, that she had fallen on her way home from school and clipped the side-view mirror of a car.

"Yes," George replied, nodding. "That's right. Fell into a car."

Adam shook his head. "My aunt tends to *fall down* a lot, too. She has similar bruises. They don't come from stairs or cars, they come from fists and feet." Adam's brown eyes, warm before, were cold now. "At first, I thought perhaps you were giving them to her." He held up his hand quickly in defense. "I know they weren't. They were from James."

"They?" George murmured, trying to remember other bruises. There had been some, on her arms, but only the one on her face.

"James," he murmured, his voice still gravelly.

Adam nodded, looking at his shoes. "I didn't really know James. He graduated this June, and wasn't in the same classes as us. The first time I really saw him was when I followed Daphne at lunch." Adam continued to hang his head.

When he raised it, his eyes shone with repressed tears. "He was waiting for her, tall, strong, good looking, everything I wasn't. So I stayed quiet instead of letting her know I was there. I should have said something. I should have told her. They kissed and hugged, and I looked away. I stopped watching for a few weeks until there was a new bruise on her arm."

George nodded. "She had a few *accidents* in the spring."

"Just the spring?" Adam asked, looking at George out of the corner of his eye.

George frowned, not liking the implication. "No, not just the spring." He thought a moment. "The fall, a year ago, there abouts. Beginning of tenth grade."

Adam nodded. "She said it started two years ago."

George stood up. His daughter had been beaten for two years by a man whose name he only learned today? He had to resist the urge to punch the siding of the house.

"It didn't start that way," Adam said with sigh. "They were friendly and happy enough at first, of course."

George sat back down. "Only one year, then." He exhaled in a snort and huff together. "One year of not seeing what was going on under my own eyes."

Adam shook his head. "Don't blame yourself. She hid it well. She didn't want you to know, or you would have. He made her keep it secret, made her promise not to tell. I blamed myself for those two weeks because I did know." Adam looked at his hands again.

"Okay, so this James has been ... what? Attached to Daphne? Dating her? How come I've never heard of him?"

"I can't answer that. I would guess, in the beginning, that Daphne was afraid to tell you. Maybe because he was so much older than her? I don't know. She never told me why, only that before long he made her promise not to tell anyone about them. I can tell you that they were ... close." Adam put a palm to his forehead, leaning into it and looking away from George.

"Close," George echoed. "He touched her." In his head, he saw hands pawing his daughter, removing her clothes. He seethed. His voice was the same volume, just colder. "He touched my baby girl, my little bug." It grew into a shout on the baby name.

Daphne came out onto the porch, throwing her arms around George's neck. He was shaking so hard he didn't dare try to hold or hug her; he would hurt her.

"I'm sorry, Daddy. I should have told you. I shouldn't have hid it. I was scared." Her voice trembled, on the verge of tears.

George breathed slowly, counting his daughter's sixteen years. When he reached fourteen, he realized that that was all she would have been when she met this ... James.

"Scared of what?" George asked. He was calm enough now that he used his hands to pull her slightly from him, to look at her face.

Daphne looked to Adam who nodded at her.

"Afraid he'd do what he did."

"Show him, Daphne," Adam urged.

She gripped her long skirt but then turned and ran back into the house.

"He didn't," George fumed. "He didn't ... rape her, did he?"

Adam sniffed and removed his glasses, his lips working. When he spoke his voice was broken and heavy with tears. "He made me watch. When he found out that Daphne and I were friends, even a little more than friends, he found us, last weekend. He came on us at the park and punched me in the face. Before I'd gotten my feet under me, he was dragging Daphne away by the arm.

"She was silent, white, looking back at me as I picked myself from the ground. I think she knew where he was going." He wiped his face on his sleeve, setting his glasses on the step. "She didn't think I'd follow. How could I do anything else?" he asked George, tears staining his cheeks. "How could I let him just take her?"

George nodded, encouraging Adam to continue. "That was our first kiss," he mumbled. He touched a hand to his mouth, closing teary eyes. "When I caught up to them, he shoved her to the ground before turning suddenly on me and wrapping an arm around my neck. I passed out."

Adam's head was in his hands now, pushing back straight brown hair. "I woke up tied to a chair. I was in some sort shed or garage, I don't know where. He had Daphne held down on the ground, her shirt torn open." Adam stopped, biting his lip hard.

"I tried to get out, but the knots ..." Adam shook his head again. "She wasn't screaming. It was like she used to it, like she knew what he was doing. The way he touched her ... She did know," Adam vowed. "He had done it before."

George didn't stop the growl that had been building since Adam related waking up.

"When he did something new, she did scream. She begged him to stop, not to take her ... her ..." Adam couldn't finish. George could fill it in. Her virginity.

"He left us there. She finally managed to get up and untie me. She begged me not to tell anyone. I tried to convince her to tell you or her mother, to go to the police."

"Her mother doesn't know?" George asked, incredulous.

Adam shook his head. "No one knows. Just me."

Eva came onto the porch again. "I think she's calmed down. What's going on out here?" Her face was lined with concern.

She deserved to know; she would know, but not now. George didn't need to tell her now. "Nothing, just a little father-daughter spat. I think she wasn't happy I didn't give her boyfriend a warmer welcome."

Eva's eyes narrowed, sensing the lie. "That's all?"

"Yeah, and Adam is fine, as you already know. I'm just ... protective," he said.

Eva nodded at last. "Well, you'll have to smooth things with her." The door closed behind George's wife before he took up the conversation again with Adam.

"I'll have his head," George growled. "On a platter. Spencer." He started thinking. He knew a Spencer, Josh.

"He's gone," Adam said softly, looking across the street rather than at George. He seemed more composed now, his glasses on his nose again. "If you're going to go after him, he left. I took a walk over there with my father, planning to call him out for assaulting me if nothing else. His father called me a lily white pencil pusher before telling me that James had left town. He said that I should have my eyes blackened a few times so I would learn how to defend myself." Adam's hands clenched at the same time as his jaw. "If my father hadn't been standing beside me ..."

George chuckled once; it sounded hysteric. "I've met Joshua Spencer. He'd have laid you flat, boy. He'd lay me flat. That man should be called Sherman, he's a bloody tank." George had worked with Josh before an accident had lamed the man. He'd heard that abusive tongue call himself and others worse things than *pencil pushers*.

Adam ground his teeth. "Still. I didn't deserve what happened to me, any more than Daphne deserved what happened to her. I filed with the police, but they didn't give me much hope."

George nodded. "Come in?"

Adam rose. "Yeah. I will need to call my mother, though."

"I'm going to try talking to Daphne," he said, thinking about his little bug crying in her room.

He climbed the stairs slowly and knocked on her door.

"Go away," she wept. "Leave me alone, Janet."

"It's not me! It's Dad!" Janet shouted. "I don't want to talk to you anyway!" The voice was hurled across the hall, from Janet's room and through two walls to Daphne, but George wagered she could still hear them. Obviously the younger sister had already tried to console the older.

The door opened a crack. "Daddy?" she asked.

"Can I come in?"

She stepped back, leaving the door open. She sat on her bed, cross-legged, clutching her pillow.

"Sounds like you had a fight with your sister." He knew he was stalling but couldn't help it.

Daphne nodded, a bit of a smile on her lips. "Yeah. She shoved her way in, so I tossed her back out. She didn't like that."

"Violence? In my house?" he asked, brows raised.

"Just wrestling," she traced a paisley on her skirt. "You aren't mad at me for not telling you?" she asked softly.

"Mad? Not really," he said, his anger all directed at the lowlife that had hurt her. "Disappointed, though. You didn't think we could help you? Protect you?"

Daphne's eyes welled with tears. "In the beginning, I didn't know I needed protecting, and then ... I didn't want you to know what he'd done to me."

George's hands balled into fists. "But I do know."

Daphne shook her head. "I didn't always try to stop him," she admitted.

"But you never wanted it, did you? He pushed you from the start," George guessed. He hoped he knew his daughter at least that well.

"I don't think so." She didn't meet his eyes. "I ... I never asked him to do those things to me, no. I didn't hate all of them. Sometimes, it felt good." When her eyes met his, he gasped, remembering the night before and making love with Eva. She had been awake and heard. How would that have made her feel?

"Last night, your mother and I ..." he stopped.

She shook her head. "That was good. I know that much. I know that when it's right it does feel good. But can it feel good when it's bad, too, Daddy?"

He really didn't want to have this talk. There had to be someone she could talk to, though. "I don't know, little bug." He pushed her hair behind her ear. "I wasn't with many women before your mother. They may not have been *right*, but they weren't *wrong* either. Damn. I want you to tell the doctor, okay? Tell him you need someone to talk to. Do you want your mom or I to make the appointment?"

Daphne shook her head. "I'll do it," she whispered. "You're right. I should have done that. Does Mom know now?"

George hung his head. "Not yet. She should know, and you should tell the police. They aren't looking for him."

Daphne sighed, putting her face into her pillow and crying again. "I know," she wept. "I know, I just ... can't. I can't live it again."

Her voice ripped his heart from his chest. She should never sound that way. Never. "It's alright, sweetheart. I'll tell your mom." He would do anything to spare her even a little of this pain. "Have your sisters met Adam? He's staying for supper."

"He is?" She brightened a little. "Oh, Dad, I think I love him. That is, if I even know what love is. I'm not sure anymore. I need him; I know that much."

George's stomach turned. His daughter in love. That should be happy next to the knowledge that had been dropped on him, but instead it added to the feeling that she wasn't his any longer.

"What did Adam want you to show me?" he asked, touching her knee.

She flinched, licking her lips. "It's already half-healed," she said, "and it isn't infected or anything ..." Pushing the pillow aside, she pulled back her skirt. A thick pinkish-red gash lay on the inside of her right thigh. It disappeared under her white cotton panties.

George closed his eyes against the red glare that seemed to fill his vision. He was going to find James Spencer; he might just kill him.

In their bedroom that night, Eva curled up to him. "Now are you going to tell me?" His smile at his wife's naked and barely dressed form evaporated. "I assumed you didn't want to talk in front of the girls. What is it, George? Something has you in knots."

He closed his eyes. "I'm headed out of town again," he said, avoiding the real issue. "There is something I have to do."

Eva propped herself up quickly, her hair dangling down her arm. "Do? What do you need to do? You just got back!"

"I'm not leaving immediately," George said softly. "You'll wake the girls. After the Manson house is up. I have to find someone."

"Find someone?" Eva's eyes were hard on his. "Who do you need to find?"

The piece of shit that raped our daughter, he thought to himself. To his wife he said, "Our daughter has been keeping something from us."

"I know Janet has fireworks in her room. She stashed them after the fourth. She wants to set them off in the winter."

George fought a laugh. It was unsuccessful. Hidden fireworks were nothing, less than nothing. "No, not Janet's fireworks. I hope you know where she has those. I don't want the house blowing up."

Eva smiled at him. "I do. They're wrapped in tissue paper in a hatbox. No risk of heat or sparks in her closet."

He nodded. "I was referring to our eldest daughter," he said soberly.

"You don't mean Adam, do you?" Eva yawned, setting her head on his shoulder. "I mean, I know she wasn't upfront about how close the two of them have gotten, but that seems harmless enough."

George stroked his wife's hair. He really didn't want to have to tell her this. "Not Adam, no. You're right, that is harmless, maybe even helpful."

He felt her smile against his pectoral as her cheek tightened. "I knew you'd like him. She has good taste."

"No," George interrupted his wife. "She ... He found her," he tried to explain. "There is another ... Adam isn't ..." How could he do this? How did he say this?

Worried, Eva sat up again to look at her husband. "Tell me, George."

"James Spencer," he said, watching her for a reaction. There was only mild confusion. "That's the name of the man who hurt our daughter, the man I have to find."

"Hurt ... I don't understand, George."

George sighed and looked up at the ceiling. "He has been involved with our daughter for two years."

"No," she said with chuckle. "Daphne would have told us. She wouldn't see a boy-"

"She was scared to tell us. She's afraid of having to go through it again telling us. Look, I told her that I would tell you, but you aren't going to believe it from me. He treated her very badly, made her think it was what she wanted, maybe even what she deserved. "

"No," Eva whispered. "That can't be true."

"Adam tried to help her. That's how he got beat up."

Eva covered her mouth, shaking her head. "No."

George pulled his wife down to him. She put her face into his chest, still shaking her head. "Shhh, Ev. Don't try to understand tonight. We can talk more tomorrow and you can talk to Daphne, okay? Just be gentle with her; remembering hurts." George remembered her shaking frame, her tears. How could he make her go through that again?

Eva didn't answer. He doubted she slept either. He knew he didn't. Every time George closed his eyes, he saw a long pink line running up his daughter's leg, and a man holding the knife.

Chapter Two

Tag had always been Lila's favorite game. Not only did she love to run, she loved to be chased. She would let her pursuer come close, only to turn and sprint away in a new direction. She didn't get to play anymore.

"Lila!" her mother would chide. "Young ladies do not run." It was worse now that her breasts had started to form. They were still small, but apparently the way they moved was indecent.

Lila didn't care. She'd seen boys noticing them and liked it. She also loved the way it felt to run.

She didn't want to run anymore, didn't want to be chased. She wished James had never noticed her, or maybe that she hadn't noticed him.

"Lila. I thought this was tag, not hide-and-seek." His voice was light and playful, but Lila knew he wasn't playing.

Hands gripping her thighs, tearing her panties away from under her skirt.

That was the first time he had caught her. He hadn't held onto her, though, his hands releasing her immediately after the loud tearing and her scream. She had run away, only to be chased again.

She had thought it was a game. When she had sat to tea with Mother, he had watched her. His smile was sweet and he was quite handsome. He was older, twenty to her fourteen. Still, she had thought he liked her, would tickle and kiss her. So when Mother had dismissed him and gone into the house, Lila had tagged him and run, hoping he would chase her.

If this was a game, she didn't want to play anymore. Her hair was tangled and full of twigs and dirt. Her arms and legs were covered in scratches. Her breath came in panting gasps, lungs burning.

He'd caught her three times, and she was sure the next would be the last. At least, she wouldn't be able to run anymore. Already, only her wits had kept him from catching her twice more. She was slowing, tripping more often, and he wasn't.

He didn't even breathe hard, his broad chest rising and falling smoothly. His sharp eyes scanned the tree line, searching for her. She could feel them when they found her. She turned and ran again through the thickest brush, snagging clothes and limbs.

She jumped a fallen log and caught her toe, falling hard in the leaf litter.

James landed atop her, knees on either side of her waist.

"Lila, Lila, Lila. You give good chase." He pulled the hair off her neck as she wept with pain into her arms.

"Please," she begged.

"Mmmm," he purred, licking her neck and ear, making her shudder with fear. "Please what?"

"P-please, let me go."

"I've always let you go, Lila. Haven't I?" he asked. His hand slid up her thigh under her skirt, where her panties no longer covered her.

"Please," she begged again.

He tsked as his hand cupped her bottom. He pressed her hip down and shifted his weight, his mouth by her ear again. "I love to hear you beg," he whispered. "You'll beg for more."

She sniffled as he reached up the back of her shirt and opened the back of her training bra. "D-don't hurt me," she begged.

"Have I hurt you, Lila?" he asked sweetly, his lips still on her ear.

She whimpered, unwilling to answer. He had groped her; he had exposed her. He had kissed her neck roughly, but he could do so much worse.

"I hope not. That wasn't my intention," he said soothingly. His hand slid to where no one had touched her before, where she knew babies and blood would come, but hadn't yet. She'd dreamed of being kissed, not ... this. She didn't want him to touch her there.

He just touched though, teasing.

"P-please," she whimpered again.

"You want that?"

"N-no!"

Too late, his finger slid inside her. She kicked one leg, but he pinned her thigh with a knee.

"Hold still," he warned in a soft voice. "It will hurt if you move too much."

She cried into her arms, willing the whole evening away.

"You must have wanted this, at least a little. Why else would you have approached me?" He pulled his hand away and backed up, sitting on his heels. A small reprieve.

She sniffled and pulled her legs under her. She couldn't run anymore. She couldn't fight him, he was too fast and too strong.

"Well? There was some reason you tagged me, Lila. What was it?"

"I-I thought you we-were beautiful. I-I thought you might l-like me." She continued to weep.

"Shhhhh." He pushed her hair back and stroked her cheek. She could smell something on his fingers and knew it was herself. She shuddered from his touch. "I do like you, Lila. Can't you tell?"

She sank a little lower, hunching in on herself, gripping her knees. They were scraped and bleeding.

25

"Oh, you poor thing," he murmured, leaning forward to kiss her broken skin. His tongue lapped at the blood still oozing from the freshest cuts.

Something in the tender kiss, the care for her small pains, made her stop cringing away from him. "James?"

When his eyes lifted to hers, his smile was predatory. "Do you have any idea how good my name sounds on your lips?" he asked. "Yes, Lila, my butterfly?" He stroked her freckled cheek and she sniffed back tears again.

"Why are you doing this?"

He closed his eyes, obviously irritated and seeking patience. "Because I want you. I want you to be mine. Mine alone." His eyes locked on hers, steady, solid, reassuring. She wasn't scared anymore. She had been taught to obey her elders, and in this moment, James' authority seemed obvious.

"Why?" she whispered, not trembling any longer.

He ran his thumb down her throat, into the collar of her blouse, popping open the first button. "Because you are beautiful. Because no one else has had you, so you can be mine completely."

She gasped. His fingers continued to work down her shirt, popping buttons all the way, popping several right off. Her bra hung loosely on her shoulders. She expected the fear to return and didn't understand when it didn't.

One hand wrapped around her throat, his thumb pressing in under her chin. "Hold very still," he warned. The other tracked up her stomach, under her bra and cupped her tiny breast, his thumb rubbing the sensitive flesh.

She moaned, part in pain, part in pleasure. His touch was gentle, but her breasts were so tender. He would feel the vibrations of her throat through his hand.

"Yes, Lila." He leaned forward, his nose alongside hers.

She closed her eyes, awaiting her first kiss. He brushed her nipple as he kissed her, making her tremble again. "You are mine, aren't you?" he asked after their first, brief contact of lips.

"Yes," she answered.

"You will never run from me again will you?"

"No," she breathed.

"Good. I'm going to let you go now. You are going to go home. When you are in your bed, you are going to think of me. And you are going to touch yourself, here." He brushed her nipple again, making her gasp. "And here." He slid his hand down between her knees, tapping her pubic bone. "I'll be watching, Lila. I will know."

She sniffled and nodded slightly against his easing grip.

"Can you find your way home?" he asked, taking his hand from her throat and pushing back her hair.

"Y-yes." She tucked her chin, trying to protect her throat. She stared at her stained skirt.

He kissed her forehead, then her nose. "I'm glad. Make me proud." Her eyes shot up to his, confused. Kissing her again, he pressed his lips more firmly to hers. "Fly, my butterfly."

He stood and turned, walking away and leaving her alone with her scrapes and tears.

Lila sniffed twice more, wiping the tears from her cheeks before standing and buttoning as many buttons as she had left. She stumbled home.

"Lila! Where have you been? And what on earth have you been doing?! Look at you!" Her mother was livid. It wasn't the first time she'd played tag in brambles and ruined clothing, just the worst. "Well, you've missed supper, and if you hadn't, you wouldn't be getting any. Into the tub with you!"

Kicking off her untied shoes, Lila made her way to the bathroom. She avoided looking in the mirror while the tub filled and tried not to see her damaged clothes as she piled them on the floor. She couldn't avoid wincing when the hot water stung all her open cuts, and her eyes were drawn to the darkening bruises all over her legs and arms.

She closed her eyes and submerged her head in the water, willing it to wash her mind clean as well.

Wrapped in a towel, she finally dared look at herself in the mirror. Her skin was red from the hot water, but not enough to hide the thumbprint on her throat, half-hidden under her chin.

"James," she whispered as she touched it. Dropping her towel, she looked at her adolescent body. Her breasts were there, that wasn't deniable. She cupped them briefly, seeing how much the flesh moved. She looked lower and saw the red hairs that had started growing above the joining of her legs. She hated them. They were ugly and coarse.

She lifted her eyes to the mirror again, looking back at herself. She saw him looking at her, his eyes in place of hers. Squeezing them shut, she grabbed towel and clothes and ran from the room.

She lay on her bed, unable to sleep. She fought tears as she obeyed his last order. Her breasts were still tender as she touched them. The saltwater leaked out anyway, and she rolled to her side, continuing to massage one breast. She touched the coarse curls forming on her sex and gagged.

There was a tap on her window and her head whipped up. There was no one there, but another tap followed, a small stone.

Wiping her face, she found her nightgown and pulled it on before opening her window. It took a minute, but she found him in the tree across from her.

He blew her a kiss before jumping down. Apparently that was enough for tonight. She lay down in her bed and wondered if it would be very bad to belong to James.

Chapter Three

George spent the next two weeks asking questions of coworkers and family friends. Fort Garland wasn't that large, almost everyone knew the Spencers in one way or another. Most didn't hold them in high esteem. The older boy had been obvious trouble, a thief. He had been arrested over the summer and was still in jail. George already knew Joshua's reputation, a hard worker with an ugly temper and foul mouth.

No one George talked to knew anything about James though. "He kept his nose clean," was all Rudy, the school janitor, could tell him. Most of the co-workers he talked to seemed surprised to hear Joshua had a second son.

"There's another one? Is he as bad as the first? I heard he's going to Kingman when he gets out, staying with Josh's family," Mick, one of the oldest men on the site, said.

George leaped on that comment. "New Mexico?" he asked. "I didn't know Joshua came from there."

"Sure," Mick answered, lighting a cigarette. "Moved here with that wife of his when he was twenty. Where were you?"

George shrugged. "Guess I was only twenty, too, and didn't care."

Mick chuckled; it turned to a hack. "Yeah, I suppose you two are about the same age. Yeah, brought that slip of a girl with him, trying to make his way. Why he came here, I couldn't guess. Not like anyone made their fortune in Fort Garland. Why the interest in Spencer? His boy take something of yours?"

"Yes," George said with a growl. "He stole something priceless. I mean to get it back."

Mick narrowed his eyes on George. "I've seen that look. You talk to the police if you need, or talk to Josh. He knows you; he'll whip it out of the boy."

"The boy's gone," George muttered, putting his eyes and hand to his task, banging a joist into place. "Over a week gone."

"Oh," Mick muttered. "Still, the cops, report it," he advised, puffing off the smoke held in his lips.

"Yeah, I'll do that," he said, considering it as he had before. The thought didn't last long. He couldn't ask his daughter to live that again, and he wanted to be sure James didn't slip through any bureaucratic cracks. There would be pleasure in doing it himself. Kingman was a good lead. If the brother was headed to family there, perhaps James had done the same. These walls were nearly finished.

After the shift, George pulled the foreman aside. "I'm not going to be able to finish this job, Joe."

"No?" he was surprised, understandably. Winter was coming and there wouldn't be another job immediately after this one. "Well, we'll manage without you, of course. You'll stay until we get the walls up?"

"Of course," George agreed. "Just have some family business to take care of."

Joe clapped a big hand on his shoulder. "Say no more. Take all the time you need." There wasn't a man here that hadn't lost a family member, broken down with wife, taken off a month when the babies came around. Work was important, but family came first. They were what made the work worth doing.

That night, he left the younger girls doing their homework at the kitchen table while he stood in front of Daphne and Eva on the couch. "I'm going to Kingman," he said without preamble.

Daphne looked at her hands, folded neatly. Eva frowned, her eyes meeting his. "How long?"

He shook his head. "As long as it takes. Daphne?" Her head whipped up as though she'd been hit. George felt bad for startling her. "Have you told your mother?"

She shifted lower in her seat. "Some," she whispered. "What I could."

Eva's jaw tightened and tears came to her eyes. She reached across the sofa, taking her daughter's hand. "You can tell me anything, sweetheart. You know that, right? You could have told me ..." Her voice trailed off as Daphne pulled her hand back.

"It's not that easy, Mom. I'm trying. I've told you what I can. I've told the doctor some, Wanda some." She straightened in her chair, holding her head a little higher. The therapist, Wanda, was helping. "I'm not sure you should do this, Dad." Her voice was calm but quiet. She had always been soft-spoken. This was the most authority he'd heard in her voice that wasn't addressed to her sisters. She railed on them from time to time.

"Why not?" he asked.

Daphne closed her mouth and chewed on her lip. "You said Mr. Spencer was strong, right? That you wouldn't fight him? James isn't as big, but he isn't small either. I don't want anything to happen to you." The fear in her eyes wasn't betrayed in her voice. "I was worried about him hurting me. I don't fear that anymore," she said with a small smile. "I do worry about him hurting you. He hurt Adam." She choked on tears, putting a hand to her mouth. "I'm sorry," she whispered, turning her head.

Eva was at her side, crouched, holding her daughter by the shoulders. "It's okay, Daph. Adam's okay. No one is hurt now, right?" Daphne nodded, sniffling. "And your Dad is trying to find him, not confront him," Eva's eyes found George, and the anger in them made his own ire rise.

He was going to confront James, all right. He was going to beat him senseless if he could. If he couldn't, then he'd find some authorities, but he'd prefer to deliver this justice with his own hands. It would be more satisfying and more permanent than anything the courts were likely to give him. Most importantly, it would save Daphne having to tell anyone else what had happened to her. He would save her reliving that if he could.

Daphne had just turned in her chair to face him when Janet and Marlene barged in, each kissing one of his bristly cheeks, saying, "good night."

"Wait, girls," he called, stopping them from running up the stairs to change for bed. "I'm afraid I have to work out of town again. I'll be leaving in a few days."

Janet's face fell a little, pouting. "Oh. Okay, Dad. How long?"

"I'm not sure, love. A month?"

Janet nodded and Marlene asked, "You'll be back for Thanksgiving, right?"

He smiled at the younger two, remembering when Daphne was as carefree as them. Looking at Marlene made his throat tight. She was fourteen.

"Yes," he promised. "I'll be home for Thanksgiving." The girls smiled at each other before climbing to their shared room.

Daphne rose to follow. "I have class in the morning. You will be careful, right, Daddy?" she asked, hugging him.

He stroked her back and kissed her cheek. "Of course, sweetheart. You know how much I love you?"

She smiled as she settled back on her heels. "Enough to find him. I love you too, Dad."

Eva stood beside him, pulling his arm around her waist. George tightened his hand on her hip, pulling her closer and kissing her temple.

"Don't worry," he told her. "I'll find him. He'll pay."

She looked up at him. "You aren't a violent man George. Are you sure you want to do this?" They hadn't openly discussed it, but since he had voiced a desire to find James, Eva had understood what he really wanted.

He sighed and leaned a little more heavily on his wife. "I know I want him to pay. I think I want to be the one to make that happen." She was right; he'd only been in a handful of fistfights, usually trying to break up drunken friends or co-workers. Never anything he had initiated, never anything cold. He was consciously choosing this. It wasn't easy for him.

James could not be allowed to get away with what he'd done. He could not bend Daphne to his will, beat her, rape her, and cast her off when he was done with her. George would not allow it. He felt the burn in his belly that came every time he remembered what had been done to his daughter.

"She didn't scream," he mumbled, remembering what Adam had told him. This wasn't one event he was avenging. Eva looked up at him in question, but he shook his head. "We have enough saved up for the winter. I won't need much more than gas. I can sleep in the car."

Eva pursed her lips and shook her head. "We're better off than that. Since the girls have been in school I've been selling my stitching. You can stay in a cheap room."

He smiled at his wife. "You're right. I shouldn't worry for you any more than you should worry for me."

"Right, so we both agree to worry anyway. Come to bed. If you're going to be leaving it soon, I want to enjoy you in it a little more." She smiled enticingly at him.

George needed no more coaxing than that. He would miss his home, his girls, but most importantly his wife. The hardest part of what he planned would be doing it alone. He wondered if she knew how much he leaned on her, used her support to keep him going.

"You know I couldn't live without you," he whispered to her as she curled onto him, sweat on her back and her breath heavy.

"I know. I need you, too," she reminded him with a kiss. "There is no family, no home, without you."

He held her tight, trying to sleep, but again, all he thought of were scars, blood, and his daughter on a dirty floor.

Chapter Four

Lila opened the door, looking around it.

A hand closed on hers pulling her into the dark room. "You came," the voice said, filling her head. "Did anyone follow you?"

She shook her head. No one in her family thought about her once she was out of sight. She met the blue eyes that haunted her nights, the full lips that felt so good against her own. She felt a tingle between her legs looking at those lips, remembering what words came from them, what they told her to do.

"Come, my butterfly," he beckoned, drawing her into a chair. He pulled her hair back from her shoulders, leaning over her shoulder to whisper in her ear. "Tell me what you've done since I saw you last."

She shivered at his breath in her ear. It still made her cringe to touch herself, but it had gotten easier. It had started to feel good. "I ... I found the bud, the one you told me about." She turned red with embarrassment.

He kissed her ear and she could feel the smile on his cheek. "Good girl, and was it all I said it would be?"

She felt tears prick her eyes. "Y-yes. It ... It was very good." She rubbed her legs together remembering how her breath caught, how that bud burned.

"Show me," he demanded. "Show me how you touched yourself, Lila. Or would you rather I do it for you?"

James' smile was sly. She didn't want him to touch her yet, it was bad enough when she did it herself. She lifted her skirt, exposing her privates. He'd told her he would destroy any underwear she wore tonight. Opening her knees slightly and licking her lips, she slid her finger up the slit.

She choked on a cry, sobbing. His breath had tingled and made her just wet enough that it slid better, made it burn. She sniffled, her eyes squeezed shut as she circled the bud with the tip of her finger.

"Very good," James praised her. Her heart filled to hear his praise, and she smiled a little, the tears slowing. His hand closed on her wrist. "Do it like this."

Her fingers softened a little, curling up, not sure what he meant to do to her, but he moved her hand up and down, focusing his touch to the bottom of the nub. She gasped, the burn so much hotter there.

"You see?" he said, kneeling in front of her, his lips just below hers. "It's good, isn't it? Who does this belong to?" he asked, stroking the back of her hand which continued in the course he'd set it on.

"You, James. Only you." Lila turned her face down. James tipped her chin to kiss her nose first and then her lips.

"Mine," he said with content. "All, only mine." His kiss heated and she squeaked, her hand stopping as his tongue was suddenly between her lips. He sighed pulling back a little. "Too much, butterfly?"

She'd heard girls talk of this kind of kiss, using tongues. She thought it seemed icky, swapping spit, but it hadn't felt icky. "N-no," she said slowly.

"That's my girl. I have more for you tonight." Remaining on his knees, he kissed her again. This time she opened her mouth, letting his tongue roam. His hand was in her hair, cupping the back of her head. Her breath was lost in his. She dared to move her tongue and felt him moan quietly. She was doing it right. She touched his lip with her tongue and he smiled against her lips, nipping her tongue in his teeth.

She yelped and pulled it back. Then she giggled, realizing he was playing. It was so hard to tell. She put her hands to his cheeks, thinking to pull him closer.

He dropped her hair, grabbing her right hand. She tried to pull it away, knowing that it had touched her. He tightened his hold painfully. She winced, knowing that she'd have a bruise later. He pulled her arm with a harsh tug.

"Whose?" he asked.

"Yours," she answered, eyes wide.

"Mine," he agreed, sucking on the finger she had used to touch herself. Her mouth worked on air, unable to understand why he did this. Then he pulled her hand down as he rose to his feet. She followed it with her eyes and jerked back, trying to free herself from his grip again.

"Whose?!" he growled.

"Y-yours," she answered, weeping. He released himself from his pants and wrapped her hand around him, closing her fingers.

"Mine," he murmured, smiling. "Also mine," he said with a smirk, pulling her hand up the length.

She sobbed, not looking as her hand stroked him.

He took her chin in his fingertips, making her look at him. He kissed her, licking her lips while still moving her hand.

"That's a good girl, Lila. Rub me like that and you'll get a nice surprise."

She sniffed her tears away, believing him. She dared look at the thick red flesh again, it was almost purple at the top where her finger and thumb ringed it. There were pale hairs curled around it. She swallowed hard, forcing herself to look.

His forehead touched hers, and his hand slipped into her hair. "That's good, Lila. Just like that," he said with heavy breath. "Would you like me to touch you?"

She jerked backward. "No," she said quickly.

Rather than squeeze her wrist again, he cupped her elbow, guiding her hand into motion again. "Then I won't. Not more than this, anyway." James' thumb caressed her cheek, and he kissed her closed eyelids. She forgot her hand was even moving as he gently traced her nose, her ears and her jaw with fingers or lips.

She noticed when it twitched in her hand. Her eyes flew open and she tightened her grip. He hissed, clenching his teeth. "Yes," he told her. "Do that."

Shaking, she was afraid of what she was doing, so scared she had hurt him and he would hurt her.

"Look closer," he said, tipping her head down.

She watched the purple head disappear under her thumb and then reappear, the slit in it opening as she pressed down.

"Unnngh," James groaned. Lila looked up as he did, so the white stream that hit her face missed her eyes.

She screamed, putting her hands to her face, sitting back.

James covered her mouth with a hand, meeting her eyes. "Shhh. Quiet, Bitch." He closed his eyes, his anger quickly controlled. "I mean, surprise. That's supposed to happen, Butterfly, just like when you get wet." He ran a hand up her thigh, making her squeak and pull her legs together.

He sighed and pulled his hand back. "You still prefer to touch yourself. That will change. You like me to touch these, though, don't you?" James' hand brushed over her blouse. She shivered at the light touch.

It was true. Once they had stopped being so tender all the time, she had loved the way his rough finger tips rubbed on them, much better than her own. His hands covered them better than her own as well, larger, broader.

He did so now, sliding around her to whisper in her ear while he fondled her new bossoms. "Lick your lips," he ordered.

She complied without thinking, such a simple request. She tasted salt and sweat, but different, thick. She gagged realizing it was what had come out of him.

He growled with displeasure. "I don't taste good?" he asked, tightening his grip, making her yelp

"I-I... yes." She reached up to her face, picking up the drop from her cheek and putting it to her lips. "Mmmm," she said, trying to convince him.

"I don't believe you," he said, "but that was a very good try." His voice was lighter. She had managed to please him. "Don't lie to me. I don't like that."

She nodded. "I will," she said, "even if I don't like it." She found a third drop to clean from her chin, licking it away.

"Excellent," James said kissing her ear. "Whose?" he asked, his tongue rounding the shell of her ear and making her tremble.

"Yours."

***

Shivering slightly in the late autumn night, Patty looked down the street. It was rather deserted this late at night. A few people came and went from a bar down the block. A few of the men looked her way and she waved. Her stomach turned as they did, not in fear or loathing. Generally a drunk john was pliable. Most likely it was hunger. She had been scraping together her earnings each night to rent a place.

Patty let out a small scream as a hand gripped her elbow and the other covered her mouth. "Who do you work for, slut?" a harsh male voice asked. The hand on her mouth retreated for her answer.

"Myself," she answered proudly, tossing long, stringy blond hair. "I'm making my own way, thank you."

Her elbow was twisted up behind her until she was lifted onto her toes; the man behind her threatened to break her arm. She'd had her arm broken once and didn't want to deal with that now; there were better uses for her money.

"I'll ask again. Who do you work for?"

Patty sighed at the familiar inevitability. She'd run from one oppressor only to be snatched by another. The delicious taste of freedom was still in her mouth and she resented having to give it up so quickly. She'd only been working these streets for two weeks. Two weeks since she'd stolen away in a delivery truck with promises of favors to the driver. Three weeks since she'd first heard that her one-time friend had left Fort Garland. Three weeks since she'd contemplated being free for the first time. Three weeks, and it was over.

"You," she answered sullenly, relaxing her muscles in defeat. If this man was like James, he would recognize her surrender and let go. If not, well, she did have enough cash for a small hospital trip. In an odd way, she preferred this. Whoever this pimp was, he didn't pretend to be her friend for three years before breaking her arm. He wouldn't take her to a movie to make up for his threat. He wouldn't pass her off to his friends ... well, actually, he probably would do that, but even then, all the cards would be on the table. There was honesty in this, honesty she had lacked before.

"That's right." He let go and Patty turned to look at him for the first time. He was oddly plain. She'd expected a pimp to be flashier somehow, a sign of his wealth. His clothes were well made, but in browns and golds, blending into the fall colors. "What's your name?"

"Patty," she answered. She heard voices behind her and turned to see the pair of men had finally come her way. "Hello," she said, trying to strike a seductive pose.

"Hey. This guy isn't bothering you is he?" the one asked.

The pimp straightened and pushed his way in front of Patty, between her and the johns. She almost grabbed him to pull him out of the way.

"I'm just keeping an eye on the goods. She's pretty, isn't she? How about a little something to make her prettier? I'll give her some, too. She'll be putting out for you all night with a little of this." The pimp pulled out a cigarette holder that was filled with tablets.

Patty felt the eyes of the men fall on her. The beginnings of a blush started, until she remembered how many boys she'd bared herself for, how many she'd fucked. There was no room for shame any more.

"Don't know that I need that," the taller of the two said, "but give her one."

Patty had no idea what the little white pill would do. She didn't trust any of these men, but if this would get her paid, she'd do it. She met the pimp's eye, one eyebrow raised.

"You're going to have a good time, Patty. Bruce'll make sure you always have a good time.

KIMBERLY GOULD

Chapter Five

George's old Ford needed filling again. He shook his head at the fourth tank, but it was the one that brought him to Kingman. He parked in front of the truck stop and went inside to get change for the phone.

"Hello?" Eva's voice came across the line.

"Hey, how's my girl?" he asked, smiling. He avoided the eyes of the other men in the truck stop that would be hearing every word of his call. They had made the same, he was sure. Still, he pulled the brim of his dusty ball cap down over his eyes.

"Missing her man," Eva answered. "No, Janet, don't-"

"Daddy!" Janet shouted into the receiver. George held the phone a little away from his ear. "How is work? Is it hard? Is it going well?"

"Work is fine," he said, hating lying to his daughter. Well if this was the work, it was going fine. It would really start tomorrow. "It's not easy," he said with a sigh. That was true enough.

"Oh," Janet said. "I hope it gets better. I love you, Dad!"

"I love you, too, Janet," he said, a little startled at the declaration, but when it was immediately followed by scuffling, he understood.

"Hi Dad," Marlene said. He could hear her smile.

"Hi Muffet. How's the tuffet?"

Marlene giggled. "It's fine, still covered in spiders."

George's smile broadened. "You still scared of them?"

She laughed louder. "You know I'm not! I miss you," she said a little more quietly.

"I miss you too, sweetie. I'll be home as soon as I'm finished, you know that."

"I do," Marlene said. "I love you. Here's Daph."

"I love you too, Muffet," he said before she passed the phone to her eldest sister.

"Hey, Dad," Daphne said. "I'm not going to talk long. Adam is over."

George's smile slipped a little, both at his daughter's tone and the knowledge that the boy held her attention during the few moments he had her. "Okay, sweetheart. Anything new? How did the appointment today go?" She wouldn't be able to say much with her mother and sisters there, but she might tell him something.

"Good," she said. "Slow. It's ... Come home soon, Dad. And safely." The concern in her voice troubled him.

"I'm being careful, little bug. Don't worry about me."

She sighed. "Right. I know. Here's Mom again."

"I love you," he said into the phone, noticing the looks he was getting.

One grizzled man with little hair, what was left was white and fine, stood with his back to George, shielding him from everyone else in the truck stop.

"I have daughters, too," he whispered, not looking over his shoulder.

"Thanks," George muttered while he waited for Eva to take the line again.

There was a pause before Eva's voice came through the earpiece. "Okay, Adam and the girls are watching Mary Tyler Moore. Where are you?"

George sighed. "I just made Kingman. It's too late to do much tonight. I'm just going to find a place to stay. You're sure we're okay?"

"Yes." Her voice was hard, too. "It's bad enough you pushed yourself to do it all in one day. You might have wrecked the truck. If you're going to keep your promise to be careful, you'll need decent sleep. I want your wits about you."

George was comforted by his wife's matter-of-fact tone. "You're right," he told her. "I'll call again when I have news." He sighed, rubbing his forehead. He planned to find that room right away, feeling more tired than hungry.

"You will," Eva assured him. "Go, sleep. I can hear how worn you are. You drove too fast, too long."

He nodded even though she wouldn't see it. "I will. God, I wish you were with me."

"You need me here, with the girls. You can always come home," she reminded him, not helping his resolve one bit.

"No, I can't." He had to do this. He had to be sure James wouldn't hurt another girl the way he'd hurt Daphne. James had to pay for what he'd done to her.

"I love you," she said sadly, knowing he wasn't convinced.

"I love you, too." He hung up slowly, sniffing hard and rubbing his nose. He turned to the man blocking his view of the truck stop diner. "Thanks," he said, holding out a hand. "George."

"Ron." Ron was missing two fingers to the second knuckle, George noticed, and the two remaining, as well as the thumb, were heavily callused. "You passing through?"

"No. I'm here looking for someone. Old family friend. Spencer?" he asked, sure he couldn't be so lucky as that.

Ron shrugged. "I'm not from here, but I bet Mae would know." He led George into the diner. As soon as the smell of the food really hit him, George knew he couldn't leave without eating. He took a seat with Ron in one of the booths.

"Mae!" he shouted. "Bring this guy some coffee. He's dead on his feet."

"You keep your voice down, you roughneck!" a raspy, but decidedly female voice, answered him. "I'll bring you coffee when I have some!"

Ron chuckled. "Mae's a good girl. Rough as sandpaper, but good heart. She can help you out. Lived here all her life, so she says. How far you come?"

George sighed, his eyelids heavy. "Ummm, Seven hundred miles?"

Ron nodded. "I go all the way from Cali to Florida sometimes. Good work for one who can't handle the finer details," he said, wiggling his hand.

George nodded. "A guy on my work crew lost his pinky. But that," he nodded at Ron's hand. "That would slow a person down some."

Ron smiled. George noticed the yellow of his teeth just before he pulled out and lit a cigarette. "I get by. Just don't ask me to write anything. I've tried learning to do it lefty. Worse than chicken scratchings."

"Here's your coffee, you loud lout. How many times do I have to tell you, this is my home, not your barn?"

Mae wore a uniform, complete with a small paper hat over her hairnet. She wasn't what George had pictured from her loud raspy voice. Her dark hair wasn't dyed, there were a few silvery strands, but it shone. She was thin, almost willowy, not unlike Eva when he'd met her. He'd been happy Eva had padded her bones some. Mae's mouth was painted red, but the rest of her make-up was sparse. She looked like she might burn Ron with her eyes alone. Eva had only looked like that once, the time Marlene had taken a fountain pen and emptied the ink on the drapes.

"Thank you, sugar. Just what I needed. And if I didn't raise my voice, how would you ever hear me in this din?" Ron's rough voice had drawn out, almost drawling; he must have been from somewhere east originally.

The charm worked on Mae. She huffed and turned to George, levelling green eyes at him. "Coffee," she said, filling the cup that was on the table. "What else can I get for you, dear?"

"Uh, beef sandwich?" he asked, not sure what he wanted.

"Dip?" George nodded. "Fries?" she asked as curtly. He nodded again. "You got it. You need anything in that pit you call a belly?" she asked Ron.

He grinned at her, showing a gap in his teeth on the left side. "Nah, I'm good with the coffee, thanks."

"I'll be back with your sandwich," she said, turning away.

"That's Mae," Ron said, watching her go. "If I weren't only here for a day at a time ..." He didn't finish the thought, but looked up at George again. "You didn't ask."

George shook his head. "Flustered. I will, though, thank you. And thanks for the phone, too. Felt like everyone was watching me."

Ron chuckled. "Like I said, I got daughters." He scratched his bald head. "Haven't seen them in five years, mind. Their mother doesn't want me seeing them. You're still with your wife, obviously."

George nodded, sipping the coffee and sighing. It was just what he needed to get him through another hour or two until he checked in to a motel.

"Well, my missus changed the locks while I was gone. Told me in no uncertain terms that I could stay with such ladies as I found on the road. I'm not missing her, be sure of that, but I do miss my babies. Violet and Carla." He sighed. "I'd show you a picture, but it's so worn out and old you wouldn't be able to make out anything from it. You got photos of your girls?"

George smiled and nodded, pulling out his wallet. "Here they are." He beamed at the photo taken the previous Christmas.

Ron used his ring finger to pull it over. He whistled. "Pretty girls. Must have to beat the boys off."

George's smile fell right off. "Actually, no. Daphne, that's my oldest, has just had her first boy over to the house. Marlene and Janet are still too young for that."

Ron nodded. "They'll bring them I'm sure. Especially this one. She's trouble." He tapped Janet.

George smiled. "Yes, she is. I miss them."

Just then the food arrived. George slid the photo back into his wallet as Mae set a plate in front of him.

George ate eagerly, dipping sandwich and fries into the au jus. Ron sipped his coffee, smiling. Mae returned as George was finishing his last fry. He sucked his fingers before licking the last of the salt from his lips.

"It was good?" Mae asked, eying the empty plate.

"Very," George said, lifting it to hand to her. "You don't have any pie, do you?"

Mae rolled her eyes. "Do you want pie, Ronald?"

"No," he pushed up from his seat, sliding past Mae and brushing her arm as he did. "I need to be going. Take care of George here. Bring him a slice of the peach." He kissed her cheek.

Mae's eyes narrowed, but he was gone before she could turn. "He always waits 'til my hands are full," she muttered. "We also have apple and blueberry, if you'd rather have one of those."

George smiled at her. "Peach is fine. I also wanted to ask you something, Mae." He wasn't sure how to go about this. It had been easy dropping Spencer's name with people he knew, and people who knew the Spencers. Mae was a stranger.

She narrowed her eyes at him and set the plate back on the table, taking Ron's seat. "My Lord, that man has a hot ass," she remarked, looking at the vinyl.

George couldn't help it; he bust out laughing. "Bet he'd love to hear you say that!"

Mae rolled her eyes. "That's not what I meant."

It took a moment, but George gathered himself. As soon as he was quiet, Mae levelled him with the same look she'd given Ron when she first came to the table. He sobered quickly.

"I saw a picture of a pretty lady."

"No!" George cut her off abruptly. "No, Mae. Shit, not that." He felt like an ass now. He should just pay his bill and go.

"Oh," she said sitting back in the booth and looking around. Whatever she was looking for she found. She pulled a pack of smokes from her apron and lit one up. "What do you need?" she asked, blowing smoke to the side.

"I'm looking for someone. James Spencer. He's not from here, but his Dad was. Thought maybe he'd come to stay with family?" George watched her for a reaction, but was disappointed. She barely blinked.

"Spencer," she said, thoughtful, taking another puff. "Why you want him?"

"I ... business," he lied.

She snorted. "No, personal. You don't lie well, George. Personal. Something to do with one of those girls?" She watched his reaction and nodded. "I have two kids of my own. I'd be out for blood if anyone hurt one of them. Sadly, I can't help you much." She squashed the butt of her cigarette and rose. "There's three Spencer families in town, and as far as I know, no one's visiting any of them. If someone were ..." she squinted, "they'd probably stay with the seniors. Ben and Mabel. You can look them up."

George caught her hand. "Thank you, Mae."

She smiled dryly. "I'm coming back, dear. You do want pie, don't you?" She tugged her hand from his grip and headed back to the kitchen.

At the bottom of George's bill was the address for Ben and Mabel Spencer.

George had no trouble finding a cheap motel. He ignored the dirty shag carpet and tugged off his boots before falling face down on the bed.

Waking with a tongue that felt like it had licked that carpet, he stumbled to the bathroom. He was happy his eyes were too bleary to see the mold in the grout until after he'd showered and shaved. He didn't care anymore then. He felt better, clean and dressed, and hoped he wouldn't scare the life out the old Spencer couple. He sat for a moment on the bed, trying to decide how he would do this.

"Have you heard from your grandson lately?" he rehearsed. "Not the one in jail, the one that rapes young girls." He shook his head. Mentioning one son was likely to bring to mind the other. Maybe he should start there.

"I'd heard that Harry Spencer was headed here when he gets out, is he staying with you? Yeah, because that doesn't sound odd coming from a complete stranger," he muttered, mocking himself. He flopped back on the bed.

What if he just watched first? If James was here, he'd be going in and out of the house. He knew a little what the man looked like, blond, tall, probably built like Joshua. He nodded at this plan. If nothing else, he could think of something to say while he waited.

Sitting on a bench, a block from Ben and Mabel Spencer's house, George watched the people of Kingman going about their day. It was a pokey sort of town, hotter than he was used to, even this late in the year. He got a couple odd looks from passersby, but not many.

He had spotted Mabel in her garden, so when she passed on her way to market, he followed a little way behind. By the end of the day, he was no closer to introducing himself, and he'd seen no one that was likely to be James.

With a heavy sigh, he went back to the truck stop to get something to eat. Mae came to his table and filled the coffee cup.

"No luck, huh?" she asked.

He closed his eyes and shook his head. "I didn't know how to ask."

She chuckled. "Yeah. 'I'm here for the guy that hurt my baby.' That never goes over well. What'll it be?"

He ordered the special off the board without really seeing what it was.

"You don't want that," she said, shaking her head.

"Mom!" he heard from the doorway followed by Mae's quiet curse.

"I've told you not to come here while I'm at work," she hissed at the seven year-old boy who was approaching. "You're supposed to be with your cousin."

"She's sleeping," he complained. "She laughed a lot, then cried a little, then fell asleep. I was bored."

Mae closed her eyes and muttered. George thought she was counting. She might have been cursing the babysitter, he wasn't sure.

"Hello," he said, extending a hand to the sandy-haired boy. "I'm George. Join me?"

Mae's eyes whipped up to find his. "You don't have to-"

He cut her off. "Please?" he asked the boy again.

"Sure! I'm Phillip. My sister is Cindy, she's working." Phillip hopped into the booth across from George, his green eyes dancing. His smile was bright.

"At least she had better be. Unlike Denise. I'm going to..." Mae continued to mutter. "You're sure you don't mind," Mae asked George.

He waved a hand at her.

"Pie's on me tonight, and I'll get you something you want to eat. And you," she looked at Phillip, poking him with a finger, "you let him eat. Don't talk his ear off."

Phillip nodded obediently, then drew his fingers across his mouth as though zipping it shut.

Mae's eyes narrowed at him, as though she were about to scold him, but her name was called from the back and she ran off.

"Mom works really hard," Phillip told George, pulling the napkin dispenser over and fiddling with it. "She has three jobs."

"Three?" George asked, surprised.

Phillip nodded. "Well, one is Avon lady, that's not quite the same, is it?" He looked up at George, seeking an answer.

"Still work," he admitted, "but not the same."

"I love it when she takes a day off. Usually it's a Sunday and we'll go down to the pool." His eyes took on a faraway look.

"What about your Dad?"

The dispenser clattered as Phillip toppled it in his surprise. "Oh, sorry." He righted it quickly and shoved it away. "He's ... gone."

George nodded. "I'm sorry to hear that."

Phillip just nodded, no longer meeting his eyes.

When Mae returned to the table, she set a plate of eggs, sausage and hash browns in front of George. It looked perfect.

"How?" he started to ask, but she was already talking to her son.

"Your aunt is at the house, dragging her good-for-nothing daughter home to sober up, I hope. You will stay with her until Cindy gets home."

"Okay," Phillip said forlornly, sliding out of the booth. "It was nice to meet you, George," he said waving.

"Phillip?" George called. The boy turned, his sneakers squeaking on the linoleum. "What are you doing after school tomorrow?"

"Homework," he said rolling his eyes and sighing.

George suppressed a snicker. "Would you mind helping me with something?"

Mae stared at George. "What?!"

"You see, I need someone to show me around town. I'm looking for some people, so I need to know where all the teenagers hang out. You wouldn't know that, would you?"

George thought he could hear Mae grind her teeth, but she didn't say anything else.

Phillip chuckled. "Yeah, I know where they go. Why do you want to go there? All they do is smoke and kiss and fu-"

"Phillip!" Mae scolded, slapping a hand over his mouth.

Phillip turned pink and covered his own mouth over her hand. "I'm sorry, Mom!" his words were muffled.

Pulling her hand away, she turned to George. "I'm not sure I want him going to those places."

He nodded. "I wasn't going to take him into any, just get him to show me where they are, in the afternoon, before they ... get exciting."

Mae sighed, but didn't argue further as George arranged to meet Phillip at the Library at three.

George woke early the next morning, hoping to see one of the other Spencer families as they headed out for work. He had two more addresses from the hotel phone book. Michael Spencer drove off in a blue Buick while Lacy stood on the step, a toddler looking through her legs. He didn't see anyone else around that house and went back to the Ben and Mabel's to watch there again.

Finally, giving up, he met Phillip at the library. He was a font of information about the town. Not the usual information, of course. He didn't know who the founding father was, or when the city hall was erected, but he knew that the log house on the hill was haunted, that the dogs in the Murphy yard were the loudest and meanest, and that if you took your bike to the spot behind the pharmacy, you could coast for three miles without turning or stopping.

He also knew all the secret hang-out spots. He led George to a bluff that afforded a beautiful view of desert. "Don't know what they come to see, it's ... desert." Phillip shrugged and turned away. He knew which farm just outside of town they usually met at after sunset. He showed George where the drive-in was, the high school, and the soda shop, though he didn't think many of the kids went there anymore. "Just old people."

George tried not to grimace. He delivered Phillip to his sister, Cindy, who was working at the table when Phillip led George inside.

"Cindy, this is George. He's cool."

Cindy rolled her eyes, also green. "You don't even know what that means," she complained.

"Do so!" Phillip argued.

"I'll see you another time, Phillip," George said, ducking out from the siblings' war of words.

"Wait!" Cindy called after him. "Mom said to give you this." She handed George a slip of paper. It had an address and a time on it. "She said something about dinner out?" Cindy raised a brow and shrugged.

George followed the address, arriving at eight, and found himself outside a steak house. He wasn't really looking to spend that kind of money, but through the window he saw Mabel Spencer chatting with her daughter-in-law. He opened the door.

"For one?" the man at the door asked.

"Uh, yeah. Just me."

"This way." He was being led away from the table of Spencers and grabbed the waiter's elbow.

"Is there anything on this side?" He cocked his head to the section where the family was gathered.

The man eyed him up and down. George groaned and pulled a five from his pocket, raising his eyebrows.

The waiter's mouth pursed and twitched, then he took the bill and led George to a table behind the family.

"Thank you," George said.

"Anything to drink?"

"Just water." The waiter sniffed. "And a nine ounce, New York, rare."

This seemed to appease the man, who nodded and left.

54

George eyed the table, taking in the three Spencers he hadn't seen before. None were younger than thirty or older than ten. He put his head in his hand. If James was in Kingman, he'd be here with them tonight.

Disappointed, he ate his steak slowly, listening to the family talk. The conversation actually came around to Harry, to George's surprise.

"We're all set for when Harry gets out in the spring," Mabel was telling Michael. "I think he'll do better here, away from Nancy and all her poison. She wasn't good for that family, mark me. I told Joshua not to marry her, but he was in love. She was awful to him, and he just took it, seemed to think that's how it was supposed to be." Mabel shook her gray head. "I thought we'd shown him better than that."

"We did, love," Ben said, kissing his wife's cheek. "Forty years worth."

"Happy Anniversary!" the woman he hadn't seen before that night said, raising a wine glass. The rest of the table followed, the kids cheering and squealing at all the clinking.

That was when it struck George. He'd always thought of Joshua as hard but fair, cold and callous. Seeing the rest of his family, he realized that the callous was built up against his wife. His harsh words and demeanour were a form of protection. And if the wife was the aggressor....

George rose, tossing a twenty on the table and hurrying out. He didn't have a reason not to be home any longer. He did fill up before he left Kingman. Striding through the diner, he found Mae and kissed her cheek. Her hands weren't full, and she slapped him.

He put a hand to his cheek but was still smiling. "Thank you," he said, turning to go.

"Wait," she called to him. "I'm sorry. You're welcome. Found what you needed?"

"No, but I know I won't find it here." She nodded and waved as he left. He started driving that night. He could be home Saturday.

Chapter Six

Lila opened her window and looked down. She knew better, but she looked anyway. The second story seemed so far from the ground. James waited for her in the tree.

"Would you rather I catch you down there?" he asked, bringing her eyes back up to his.

"N-no," she stammered. Climbing into the window, her bare toes on the sill, she crouched. The back of her head brushed to top of the opening. She wore little, a filmy nightdress, but he had coat and boots for her as soon as she landed the jump. It was the chilliest it would get, the middle of December.

"I'll catch you," he promised. "I don't want you hurt," he reminded her. "You are too precious, my butterfly. You can fly, like one, show me!" He smiled and she was charmed by it, believing him.

Even though he pressed her to do things she didn't want to, eventually she came to enjoy them. She was beginning to think he was bringing out some hidden part of her, making her shine more brightly. Certainly her mother seemed to think so, complementing her on her choices in clothes and style of hair, priding the posture she was developing and the sway in her step.

"You will be a fine lady, a lovely wife," her mother had said, kissing her cheek at one of her Sunday teas. James had been there and his look had shown equal pride. He still kept his distance from her at those public gatherings and warned that she shouldn't tell her mother about him. He was far too old for her. Still, he promised he would talk to her parents when she was a little older, sixteen.

Lila was buoyed by the memories of praise, and launched herself from the window, a fluttering streak of white in the moonlight.

James caught her around the chest and waist, pulling her with him into the magnolia. The branch shuddered and creaked; he staggered and fought for balance. Eventually, everything was still except for Lila's slight tremble. She heard her teeth chatter the same moment he did.

"Shit, don't get sick on me," he said, pulling her coat down from a branch he'd hung it on. Placing it on her shoulders, he pulled the hood up and kissed her lips. "It wouldn't do to ruin our date with coughing and fever."

She shook her head in agreement. He spaced out these nights enough that by the time they came, she was eager for them. He still watched through the window every night, or nearly every night, and she was vigilant in her efforts to please him by pleasuring herself. She tried not to think of the small scar on her lower back, the mark left from the night she didn't.

She still didn't know how he'd gotten into her room, but in the morning there was blood on her sheets. Her mother, thankfully, had assumed her period had started and explained by giving her a package of napkins. Her period had actually started a few weeks later, so she was glad to have them then, but the blood in her bed had come from a small gash on her back above her waist.

He didn't want her hurt, and he tried not to hurt her, but sometimes his passion got the better of him, causing him to hold her too tightly, or grab her too hard. Had he cut her? She had no way to be sure. She had been fast asleep but she had no other explanation. She had been careful to always do her best when he was watching.

She'd started touching herself when he wasn't watching, too, in the bathtub mostly. Her older brother had caught her at it, breaking into the bathroom without knocking. He'd turned scarlet and not talked to her for a week. When he did, he pretended he'd seen nothing, though he pulled her aside one evening and told her to be careful with boys.

She'd laughed it off, but Christian insisted, warning her that boys sometimes told girls nothings just to get them into bed. Lila had told James all about Christian's warnings. James hadn't been happy but wasn't angry with her, asking if she thought that he was telling her nothings.

As she climbed down the tree, she told herself that she meant too much to him. He held his hands over his head, helping her down the rest of the way, and then keeping hold of her so that her weight didn't fall completely on the cold ground until she had her boots on. He didn't want her hurt; he didn't want her to catch cold. That was different from the boys her brother warned of. She was sure they didn't have a care for the health of the girls they lied to.

James took her hand and kissed it, then he kissed her and led her away to the outbuilding behind his aunt's home. It was their hidden nook, where he'd often brought her before. His lips were hot on hers before the door even closed.

"Lila," he breathed. "You are an amazing girl. How can others not see it?" He murmured, his lips finding her neck as he lifted her onto the small mat he had laid on a table for a bed.

She wrapped her ankles around his waist, kissing him in return. Her hand automatically drifted between her thighs, but he caught it, pulling it to him. She redirected quickly, slipping it into his pants.

His eyes blazed as she held him. "Not what I'd intended," he said in a near-growl. "Not that I don't appreciate it."

"Oh," she murmured, letting go. She still felt awkward holding him, much more so than touching herself, as she did it less often. He was so big in her hand.

"Lie back," he said, holding onto her wrist.

She obeyed, her flame colored curls pooling around her head as she looked up at the rough wooden beams of the old smoke shed. She nearly jumped off the table when she felt not his fingers, which she'd started to become accustomed to, but his lips on the inside of her thigh. "No!" she said, sitting up.

"Whose?" he asked, squeezing her wrist as he bit lightly on the skin inside her leg.

She winced and lay back, fighting tears. "Yours," she said.

"That's my girl. You're going to enjoy this." He used his fingers as he had before, brushing the skin of her sex. Her breath fell into the familiar pant and gasp that came from him touching her, much less controlled than the heavy breathing she used when she touched herself. She didn't know when he would brush the bud at the top, when he'd circle lower. To this was added not knowing when and where he would kiss the inside of her thighs.

She relaxed the longer he went without putting a finger in her, that was still uncomfortable for her, although, it was getting better each time. Just when she thought she might burst from sensation, a new one was added, not a finger, something softer, wetter.

"James?" she asked, feeling her legs tense. "What? Oh!" she lost the train of thought as whatever he had placed inside her moved deeper and then out entirely.

"My tongue, my sweet. And very sweet you are." She propped herself up just enough to see his blond hair, but she shook as he licked hard up her sex, spreading it open. Her head thudded on the table. "Is it as good as I promised?" he asked, his tongue entering her again.

Her legs twitched on his shoulders and she felt more movement inside her. Was his tongue doing that? When he withdrew and the rippling continued, she knew it couldn't be him. It was her.

"Yes, but what is happening?" She didn't understand as she lifted her hips to the tongue that was now playing with the nub at the top of her, the one that was so sensitive to touch. She squealed and bit her tongue. James covered her mouth lightly, then gave her a kerchief.

"Scream into that," he suggested. It was unlikely his family would hear her in any case, but she wadded up the cloth in her fist and stuck it to her mouth, letting herself scream as he continued to use his tongue on her. She still didn't know what was happening. It was more than the shuddering shock that often came when she touched herself for a long time. It was more than the painful squeeze she had sometimes given his fingers. This made her see red and thrust her hips up and out.

She noticed he had stopped licking her, holding his tongue in place while she moved, and slowly, she stilled. Gasping for air, she pulled the bundle of cotton from her mouth. "What was that?" she begged of him, sitting up.

He smiled brightly and she noticed that his face gleamed in the faint light from the moon. He pulled a finger over his jaw and put it to her lips.

Her eyes widened as she recognized the scent. "All of that?" she asked, licking his finger obediently.

His grin was flawless as he nodded. "That, my butterfly, was beautiful. Your first full orgasm." He kissed her now, holding her close, hands sliding over her back, her sides, and then up into her hair. His tongue entered her mouth, sharing the taste with her.

She didn't have to fight being sickened by her own scent any longer, she'd grown so used to it. He'd made her clean his fingers before, of course. She reached down and he grabbed her hand again.

"Do you think you can return the favor?" he asked, eyes intent on her.

Her jaw dropped. He wanted her mouth on him? Her hand barely wrapped around.

"I will do my best," she promised, knowing she would fail, afraid of what would happen when she did.

"I know you will," he agreed, helping her down from the table and taking a seat in the only chair in the room. He opened his pants and freed himself for her. Taking the hand he still held, he wrapped it around the base of him. "You will do fine," he promised her.

She was sure he was wrong, but she bent anyway, kissing the dark purple knob that topped his member. Her back protested, and she settled onto her knees.

"Easier that way?" he asked, pulling her hair to the side. "I should have told you."

She smiled. "Yes, easier. I ... what do I do?" she asked, looking up at him and slowly stroking. She had learned how he liked to be held, but how could her tongue do anything like that?

"Suck," he said, pulling her head down slightly, until her lips touched him. "Open your mouth and suck like you would on a Popsicle.

She usually licked Popsicles, but she thought she understood at least. He was still too large. She opened her mouth and stopped. His hands tightened on her, a sign of irritation.

She licked up the length quickly, the way she would enjoy the icy treat, and his hands twitched, his eyes closing. "Yes," he hissed.

She sighed in relief and licked him again, along a different edge this time. Then she tried what he suggested. Opening her mouth wide, she slid him over her tongue. His hands pressed to her scalp and started pushing.

She struggled, trying to pull her head back up, fighting for air. It came up quickly as he abruptly let go. "Shit! Fuck! You bit me!" He slapped her across the face.

She put her free hand to her cheek, tears stinging her eyes. His face softened from anger to sadness. "Oh, Butterfly. I'm sorry, but that hurt," he told her, kissing the cheek that still smarted. "I didn't mean to slap you."

She nodded, believing him. "I didn't mean to bite. You ... I couldn't breathe," she tried to explain.

"Of course," he muttered. "Have to go slowly, don't we? Try again?" he asked, pulling her chin down.

She really didn't want to. Just this moment, she wanted nothing more than to be back in her bed.

"Lila?" he asked in a harsh tone. "Try again." He didn't ask this time, and she thought he might push himself into her mouth. Would she bite him if he did? Would he hurt her?

She took a deep breath, gathering courage, and tried again. She was able to breathe through her nose this time as she worked a quarter inch at a time into her mouth. It was slow progress, and he pulled her up to make her start again from time to time, his shaft sliding in and out over her tongue. She did her best to keep her teeth from him, but he pulled her hair and hissed more than once when they scraped. She had tears in her eyes by the time she felt his hair against her nose. Was this what he had wanted? Had she succeeded?

"Yes, Lila," he moaned, pulling her back part of the way only to push her down again. It hadn't been as aggressive as that first time, never choking her, but she did gag now, taking him so deep in her mouth, into her throat. "Fuck," he groaned and held her in place.

She fought to keep her jaws open, but her hands balled into fists and beat on his thighs as she felt the pulse that meant he would release sperm on her. Tonight it would all be in her mouth. She choked as it came and he let her up only enough to swallow, coughing around him.

"That's it," he said, pushing up into her face one more time. "Drink all of that, Lila."

She wept but didn't choke this time, licking him clean instead, as she did when the white goo landed on her.

"I need to get you home," he murmured, "but I think I need to hold you first. Is that alright, Lila?" He pulled the weeping girl into his lap and kissed her curls as he smoothed them. "That was very good for your first try. I'm still sorry I slapped you."

"I know," she answered. "I'm sorry I wasn't better." She meant it, too. She wished she could remember all the nasty things her classmates had said about doing things like this with boys, it might have helped. She still avoided those girls, however, not liking the way they behaved or looked. She wasn't like them, was she?

James rocked a little as he held her on his lap. "I love you, Lila. You will be mine, forever."

She sighed. She liked him best this way, gentle and soothing. He didn't soothe her often, but he was very good at it when he did. Her eyelids grew heavy.

***

Patty looked up into the cool eyes of the man whose dick was in her mouth. He would pay her, in the drug she so desperately wanted. The tab that would erase the pain, erase the shame. Nothing could touch her once that hit her system. She would be on a cloud. She would be a cloud. She would suck all the cocks in the world to get it.

There was a freedom that came with the drug, a control in the lack of control. She was choosing to take it, just as she chose what she ate, or more often didn't eat. It was a new freedom to replace what she'd lost when Bruce became her pimp. He told her who to fuck and when, but aside from that, he left her alone, knowing the need for payment would keep her from wandering too far. Bruce was infinitely preferable to James.

It had taken a week to believe James really was gone and weeks more before she stopped looking over her shoulder every time she did something he wouldn't approve of. The pinnacle had been leaving Fort Garland, leaving the family that had never paid much attention to her, one more brat in the pack. Unlike her family, she had been sure James would notice and appear when she jumped into the cab of a truck headed to Fort Collins. If he had, he would have hurt her badly enough that she wouldn't be able to run. When he didn't, she had laughed. Her first laugh in a long time.

Patty had hoped she would be forgotten when James had found Daphne. That would have suited her. He hadn't of course. He still wanted his homework done for him, among other things. He didn't look at her the way he looked at Daphne, but he still wanted to know where she was, who she was speaking to, and made sure she didn't say anything to anyone. He still wanted her at his beck and call, but he didn't want to touch her, except to hurt her.

James talked to Patty once about Daphne, about how she was a real woman and could be a real wife. Patty had known she wasn't worth marrying, but she thought she was at least worth a fuck. Not to James Spencer, though. No, he'd left her to be picked over by their classmates. He'd been interested in watching that, for some reason. Probably just to see her further debased. It wasn't like she could get a whole lot lower.

She shifted, exposing the scars on her leg, all from James' knife. Each one a reminder that she would do as he said, when he said, or he'd do worse. Each one a reminder of how low she was, how far under his thumb. Sure, he followed them up with sodas and smiles, matinee shows, all the things she'd come to enjoy doing with him, all the things that had made him her friend in the first place.

Bruce had given her only two scars, and both were from the ring he wore, not a knife. He didn't want to damage the goods, but a punch or kick in the middle left marks only seen long after the deal had been made. She'd earned fewer punishments than the girls she worked with. It never occurred to her to lip him off like the other girls did, to say no. What Bruce wanted was never terrible, and the payment ...

James wasn't here, and Bruce was. She had a job to do, a job that would pay her what she needed. Pushing James out of her mind, she worked her tongue harder on the dick she was sucking, stroking the man's balls and the base of his shaft.

"That's it, Patty. God, you're good," he groaned, pulling her face down over him, his hair tickling her nose.

She choked it back, the burn of bile familiar and ignored. How long since the last time she'd made herself vomit?

She'd thought, maybe, if she looked more like Twiggy or the other girls on the magazines, James would want her for more than a buddy, more than a punching bag. It had started with purging, keeping her hunger down while appearing to be eating. That hadn't lasted long. Soon she just stopped eating. No one watched her closely enough to notice she never had lunch, and her family didn't miss her at dinner. There was never enough for all of them. In fact, part the reason she'd stopped purging was because her family couldn't afford food for her to throw up.

The boys in her class noticed when her already sparse baby-fat fell off completely. The boys had been quick to want her then, and James had been happy to let them have their turns. He just made sure they all understood that she was his first, even if she wasn't for fucking. That hurt most when she knew he was touching, if not fucking, Daphne.

Well, the purging had come in handy. She'd done it enough that her gag reflex was almost non-existent, which the johns appreciated.

"Yeah," he hummed, placing a white tab on his tongue before passing one to her. "You earned it, baby. I haven't been blown like that ... I've never been blown like that."

A compliment, even for a blowjob, was foreign to her. Bruce sometimes commented to himself that she was a money-maker, but not a real compliment.

"I didn't get your name," she asked, just before putting the tab on her tongue. Once she did that, she'd neither hear nor care.

"No names, sweetheart. But trust me, I'll be back." He pushed her finger toward her mouth. She wasn't slow to join him in the bright-lights and floating feelings that followed. He may have fucked her again, he may have left her in a gutter. It didn't matter. She didn't matter.

Chapter Seven

Daphne continued to show the scars of James' touch. George watched from the kitchen as Adam kissed her goodnight and tears sprang to her eyes.

"No," she begged him when he pulled away, "don't stop. Make me yours."

George's stomach had turned at that, and he might have stepped out to intervene if Adam hadn't pulled her into a hug instead.

"You aren't mine, Daphne. And you aren't his either. You are yours. Isn't that what Wanda tells you?" he asked, stroking her brown curls.

Daphne sniffled and nodded, gripping Adam's waist tightly. "She does."

"I'm happy with what you're ready to give, Daphne. I'm not going to take you like he did. Only what you give," he murmured, continuing to console her.

She wept more loudly. "I want to give you more, I do. He won't let me." She shook her head, backing up and putting her hands to her hair.

Adam grabbed her shoulders, tugging her hands down. "You aren't his. He will never touch you again, Daphne. He can't hurt you anymore. I'm so sorry." He kissed the top of her head, hugging her to his chest. "I'm sorry."

"I'm sorry," she whimpered. "Kiss me again?" she asked, looking up at him. The porch-light reflected off her tears.

Adam complied, kissing her gently, brushing her lips with his own. She sighed and eased up visibly.

George stormed up to his room and violently removed his clothing. He had to find James Spencer. He had to make him pay.

Finding himself without work early in the new year, George threw himself into the search. He had discovered that Nancy Spencer was one of six sisters from Flagstaff, Arizona. At his request, the public library had brought in archives of the Arizona Daily Sun. After days of scrolling through microfilm, he had the names of all five of Nancy's sisters and the men they had married.

Not long after that discovery, Joe had called with a new project in town, a renovation. George had to set his search aside, but it was never far from his mind. As a result, he grew more and more irritable as the months dragged on. He was getting less and less sleep, plagued by nightmares. As he learned more pieces of what Daphne had endured, delivered through the medium of her therapist when she couldn't say it herself, his dreams became more vivid, more disturbing.

He still remembered the round gray-haired woman, sipping her tea while telling him, at Daphne's request, the atrocities that had been delivered upon his daughter. George didn't know if the tea was to hide her own discomfort on the topic, or to put him and Eva at ease. Her voice was calm and level as she explained that Daphne had been taught slowly, over two years, to touch herself, to touch James, to not let anyone else touch her. George shivered remembering how coolly Mrs. Peterson had given them the details of James' power over their daughter, details Daphne wasn't able to share on her own.

It wasn't long after Wanda Peterson had told him about James' conditioning that George noticed Daphne's hand straying to her lap when she sat with Adam. Her boyfriend always spotted it quickly and twined her fingers with his, holding her hand.

George's self-hatred grew. How had he let this happen? Why wasn't he able to do anything to fix it? Why couldn't he find one of those sisters? Why did work take him from this task that was so important, vital?

Five months after his revelation in Kingman, George had found only one of the sisters. He hadn't made plans to go to Jackson, yet. Easter was approaching and there was a lot of work in town. Spring storms had brought a flood of roof repair jobs. He knew his family needed that money, probably more than they needed him to track down James, as much as that hurt to admit.

Janet came over with a Sears' catalogue. "Daddy? Can I get this dress for Easter?"

He looked at the price and cringed. "No, Janet, we can't afford that."

"But I thought, with all the extra work you've been doing ..."

"I said no!" he snapped, feeling liquid slosh over his wrist. He looked at his hand, at the tumbler of Pepsi and whiskey he held. He closed his eyes and took a deep breath, setting the shaking glass on the end table next to him. "We still can't afford that dress, Janet." She didn't know he hadn't been 'working' over the winter.

"O-okay," she stuttered; not afraid, but obviously startled by his vehemence. "I can wear one of Marlene's dresses. Do you think I could have new shoes?" she asked instead.

Sighing again, he forced a smile. "Maybe. Why don't you look at some?" he suggested, pointing to the catalogue she had dropped to the carpet.

She nodded and lifted the book, sitting back on the couch with her sisters. Marlene was the only one not staring at him.

George stood, taking his glass with him to the kitchen. He poured the brown liquid down the drain. It wasn't helping.

"Dad?" Daphne's voice had always been soft, but George wondered if she'd gotten even quieter.

"Yes, sweetheart?" he asked, not turning from the sink.

"You aren't sleeping, are you?"

"No more than you," he answered. He had heard her crying in the night, heard her drifting through the hall on the nights he didn't.

"I think you should visit Wanda."

Eva had started her own sessions with Daphne's therapist soon after Adam and Daphne. Eva's guilt had seemed even greater than his own, but it had faded with the visits. His wife was actually sleeping, something he still couldn't manage. She had suggested the same when he rolled out of bed in the dead of night.

"So does your mother," he muttered, looking into the drain. When would he find time to see a therapist? What would his co-workers say if they knew?

Daphne came and hugged him from behind, resting her cheek on his shoulder blade. "He doesn't hurt me anymore, Dad. You don't have to push yourself this hard."

He turned carefully, wrapping an arm around her and tucking his little bug into his side. "I do. I'm going to find him, Daphne, but I'll also call Mrs. Peterson."

"Good," she said with a small smile, stretching to kiss his cheek. Her kiss was followed by two others. Marlene first and then Janet.

"I'm sorry I made you angry, Daddy," she apologized.

"Oh, love," George said, seizing her into a hug and then tickling her ribs, getting kicked in the process. "I'm not angry with you. I love you."

"I love you, too. Good night, Dad."

Eva stepped in after them, taking his hand and leading him upstairs behind the girls. "It's not going well?" she asked, rubbing his back and standing beside him.

George turned and leaned against the counter. He crossed his arms, his forehead creasing. "No. I ... have hit a wall." He pulled out his wallet and fished for the scrap of paper he never went without. It was the list he'd made from wedding announcements. "I have all the names, but none of the places."

Eva took the paper from him. "Let me do this. I can spend all day at the library. You focus on work and sleep. Just so you're warned, I intend on tiring you out enough to sleep tonight." Her eyes left no question as to how she would do it. He felt his blood racing just from that gaze.

"Thank you," he said, looking at the paper in her hands.

"I'm just glad to be able to help! It feels like I haven't done anything." She looked at the list, tears filling her eyes.

George hugged her, kissing her temple. "You *have* helped me, been there for the girls. You do plenty."

She huffed, not accepting that. "Well, I can do this." She found her purse and put the list away. Pulling him from the counter, she turned on a radio, urging him to dance with her. "Come," she pleaded, "until the girls are asleep."

He turned with his wife in his arms, never graceful, but moving as she did.

A few hours later, she was perched atop him, her hair framing both their faces. She was close, holding against the climax that was claiming her. She felt so good on him, but every time he started to give in to the pleasure, his mind went to Daphne, asking Adam to kiss her, to claim her, and the edge was gone from him. He stayed hard, just ... couldn't. This wasn't Eva's first orgasm tonight, and she was frustrated that she couldn't give him the same.

"Please, George," she begged now, rippling around him as her entire body tightened. "Come with me." She let out a stifled cry and he pulled her to him, thrusting deeper into her, holding her through the peak. Relaxing on him, she sighed. This time, he lost rigidity and slipped from her. She seemed to take this as a sign that she had finally succeeded. "Thank you," she murmured. "Sleep."

George kissed her head. "Yes, sleep." He didn't, simply holding her and listing Nancy's sisters in his head over and over. He would find James; he had to.

***

Wanda Peterson's voice was slightly nasal. "Hello?"

"Hi. This is George Kingston."

"Mr. Kingston," she said. "Wonderful of you to call. How can I help you? Daphne has been progressing well, but I don't have anything new to tell you."

"No, I'm ... calling for myself."

"I see," she said. "As you know, I don't normally accept visitors after five, but I can make an exception for you, if that would be easiest?"

He sighed. It was bad enough calling from a payphone just off the job site. At least he didn't have to skip out on work. "That would be great," he answered gruffly.

"I'll see you tonight, then. Six?"

"I can be there at five," he told her, not wanting to strain her schedule too far.

"Five o'clock," she agreed. "Enjoy your day."

He managed through the rest of the shift, narrowly avoiding falling off a roof and dropping a load of shingles on Mick. He didn't avoid hitting his thumb, twice. There wasn't anyone on the site that wasn't glad to see him leaving.

He knocked on Mrs. Peterson's door and was asked to come inside.

"Mr. Kingston," she said, rising and shaking his hand. "So good of you to come." She wore a red scarf tied around her head which stood out against the gray hair. "Please, have a seat. Tea?" she asked, pouring herself a cup.

"No thanks," he mumbled, feeling bad about sitting on her nice sofa in his dirty work clothes.

"Really, sit. Don't worry about it." She motioned with one hand, doctoring her tea with the other.

George sat, fiddling with his ball cap. Where did he begin? What should he say?

"How is your wife?" she asked, sipping from her cup.

"Oh. She's good. Really good. She was beside herself there for a while, but talking to you seemed to help a lot." He wiped a hand across his forehead and grimaced at what he found on his palm. Digging out a kerchief, he wiped again.

"I see." Mrs. Peterson tapped her teacup with one nail, eyes narrow. "How is Janet?" Her smile returned.

"Janet," George said, startled. "Um, good. Very good. Her classes seems to be going well. Haven't heard a bad word about her, or out of her. Janet is a good kid. Even if she did stash fireworks in her closet. Made for a colorful New Year," he said with a grin.

Wanda smiled with him. "Yes, Daphne told me about that. Nearly had a burning bush?" She chuckled and George laughed with her.

"Nearly." He sighed. "I'm not sleeping," he said bluntly. "Every time I stop for a moment, I remember what he did to Daphne. Then I go back to searching for him."

Mrs. Peterson pursed her lips. "George? Let's talk about something else first."

"But this is the problem," he insisted.

"I know, but we need to hit it from the side, if you will. You work with buildings?" she asked.

"Yes."

"Well, think of it like trying to barge through a locked door when the window is open."

He nodded, thinking he understood.

"You focus on the search. How is that going? You didn't have any luck in Kingman?" She sipped the tea.

"No. Well, yes. I learned that Nancy is the reason Joshua is the way he is. Seeing the Spencer family, hearing them talk about Harry coming to stay with them, it made it clear that Josh was a different man when he was younger."

Wanda nodded. "Joshua is James' father, I assume, but who is Harry?"

"Oh, sorry. Yeah, Josh and Nancy are the parents. Harry is James' older brother. He was locked up for grand theft auto. He's ... well, actually, he would have just been released," George mused. That meant he'd be in Kingman now. Maybe he should call Mae ...

"I see. Daphne didn't know much about his family, and Eva and I ... well we didn't talk about James very much at all." She set the cup on its saucer and regarded George. "You seem very animated when you talk about the family and what you've learned so far."

"Yes. I'm going to find him."

"Why?" she asked.

George was dumbstruck. It was obvious, wasn't it? "To make him pay."

"How do you plan to do that?" Wanda asked, pouring herself another cup from the teapot on the table between them. "Are you sure you don't want a cup?" she asked, holding the pot.

"No, thanks," George repeated. "You don't have coffee? Or a Pepsi?"

"Sorry, no." She smiled as she added sugar to her cup. "You plan to take justice into those well-worn hands?" she asked, looking at his fingers.

He clenched them into fists, over the table. "Yes."

"You think that will help Daphne?" Wanda wasn't looking at him, setting the teapot in a precise location, turning the handle just so.

"I ... no, I don't imagine it will help her at all."

"So you are doing this for you."

George's jaw went slack. He didn't know what to say. She was right.

"There's nothing wrong with that, George. I think you might be equating the two though, when they aren't actually related." She sipped her tea again. "Your need for vengeance is separate from Daphne's pain. Both need to be addressed. Both deserve your attention."

He looked at the flowery teapot, unable to meet the therapist's blue eyes.

"George?" she asked and he looked up reflexively. "Are your problems stemming from hers, or are they your own?"

He looked back at the pot. "They're my own."

She reached over and touched the back of his hand. "Would you like to come see me again next week? I can stay after five again."

He nodded, unable to answer.

"Good. Then we can start working on your problems, or we can talk more about Daphne's and how you can help her. Eventually, we will address both."

He nodded again. "Eva is helping me search."

"Good!" Wanda said, setting down her cup with a clink. "That's great. Lack of progress has been troubling you, hasn't it?"

He nodded.

"We can talk more later if you want time to think," she told him, touching his hand again.

"I ... would. Will I sleep tonight?" he asked, then started. "I mean ..."

Wanda closed both hands on his. "I think you will, George. I think even this will be progress enough to allow you that."

He sighed, feeling relieved already. "You're good," he murmured.

"So I've been told," she said with a smile, looking at the pictures that sat on her book shelf.

George looked at them now. Men, woman, old, young, they seemed to have nothing in common, except Wanda Peterson.

Eva knew that George would be late, so supper was just being set on the table when he entered. He noticed six place settings as well as Adam's shoes in the doorway. He was growing more and more accustomed to having him around.

"How did it go?" Eva asked quietly. Marlene was spooning potatoes into a bowl but didn't seem to hear.

"Good. I'll tell you about it tonight."

"I'm glad," Eva said, kissing him. "I have news for you, too." Her eyes sparkled, and he was instantly curious.

Just then, Janet ran from the living room, tackling him in a hug. "You're home!" she cried. "Why were you late?" she asked, pouting.

"Janet," Eva scolded. "Your father doesn't need to account for his every moment with you."

The adolescent looked down, abashed. "I'm sorry. I missed him," she whined, then hugged George again.

He grunted a little. "I wasn't gone that long."

"I know," she frowned. "Sometimes it feels like you're away even when you're home."

George sighed. He really had been preoccupied. "Hopefully that won't happen so much anymore," he said, hugging Janet back.

"Good." She squeezed him again and they sat around the table.

George sat at the table with Eva after the younger girls had gone up to bed. Adam and Daphne were on the porch, saying their good nights.

"What good news?" he asked, unable to wait any longer.

"Winifred and Charles live in Santa Fe. I even have their phone number." She smiled and pulled a slip of paper for him.

"You already found one?" he asked, surprised. "How? I ..." He suddenly felt terribly inadequate. Quashing the emotion, he hugged his wife around the shoulders. "Why didn't I ask you to help sooner?"

She shrugged. "I have no idea. Does this mean you'll sleep tonight?" she asked with a grin. "I noticed you didn't last night." It turned to a scowl.

"I think it does. This is for me," he said, looking at the paper in his hands, "not Daphne. Maybe it'll help some other girls, but it won't help her." He hung his head, feeling selfish.

"Do it for them, for the other girls." Eva kissed his cheek. "Do it for yourself. I can't say I understand completely, but it's clear you need to do this. We'll make sure you do."

He nodded. "So ... should I just call and ask for James?" he joked looking at the number at the bottom.

"Sounds like a good idea to me," she said with a smile of her own. "You can always claim wrong number."

He chuckled. They both quieted at the sound of raised voices on the porch. Daphne almost never raised her voice.

"How can you expect me to be honest when you aren't?" Her quiet voice was hard.

"They don't need to know-" Adam spoke over her.

"Yes, they should," she retorted.

"What he did to me is nothing, nothing compared to-"

"How can you say that?!" Daphne's voice was loud and clear now. She must have realized because she hissed the next words. "Just because your scars are physical and fully healed doesn't make them any less important." George wasn't positive he heard that right.

Adam sighed, his words too low for Daphne's parents to hear, but her sigh was a little happier.

"We probably shouldn't listen so closely," Eva told him, smiling. "Take me upstairs?"

George wasn't sure she'd be any more successful at getting him off tonight. He hadn't progressed far enough for that, but it never hurt to try. As the sound of kissing came from the door, followed by Janet's cry of "gross!" he felt even better.

Chapter Eight

James continued to meet Lila's eye across the table. It was the first tea of the year that Lila's mother had held outdoors, and the first in several that James had attended.

"Lila," her mother snapped. The girl looked up, unsure what she might have done wrong. "Bring out another plate of sandwiches?"

Oh, she hadn't been keeping an eye on the refreshments as she should. She rose and entered the house. The door opened again behind her. She looked over her shoulder just in time to see James. His hands came around her waist, toying with the white lace of her dress and lifting the skirt.

Lila's hands, filled with the platter, twitched. "What happened to tonight?" she asked, half-giggling.

He growled in her ear, making her shiver. "Tonight, too. She doesn't need those now, does she?" He took the tray and set it back down, lifting Lila's skirt in back, rubbing his hardness against her. "You can spare a few minutes. She won't even miss you now that you're gone."

His words struck a little too close to home. It was true that her mother seemed to have no mind for her once she was out the room, and only criticism when she was. Still, she really shouldn't linger here.

"James," she whispered, turning her head to look over her shoulder.

His mouth found hers, hungrily pulling on her lips and tongue. She gasped at his fervor. His thumbs were sliding her panties down.

"No, James," she murmured. "Not like this."

"Just like this," he answered, and she heard his belt jingle as he unfastened it. "Whose?" he asked, rubbing one hand between her legs.

She bit off a scream. "Yours," she said through clenched teeth.

"Mine," he growled, pressing himself against her. He hadn't done this. She knew they shouldn't do this, not now, not here.

There was a clatter of the door opening and James pulled down Lila's skirt, moving behind her and fiddling with his pants.

"Lila!" her mother scolded. "I'm sorry, James, didn't she direct you? The washroom is through there." She lifted one white-gloved hand to show him.

"Thank you, Ma'am." James' drawl hadn't taken long to develop, and now he sounded like all the other young men in Knoxville.

"You." Lila's eyes widened at her mother's tone, and she clutched the platter to her. "You had best not have offended James Spencer. His aunt is one of the more influential women in my circle."

"No, Mother. He wasn't offended. I'm certain." Lila's eyes darted briefly in the direction of the bathroom.

"Good. Get those sandwiches out there."

Lila took one hand from the platter as she crossed the mudroom to adjust her skirt and hitch her panties up. That had been too close. She needed to be clear with James. If he wanted that, he was going to have to speak to her parents. She had turned fifteen; that was surely old enough for an engagement. Her own mother had gotten married at sixteen after all.

That night, Lila tiptoed down the stairs. She had heard her parents in their bedroom but didn't know where her brother was. Out with friends, she was certain. James waited for her just outside the door.

"There is my butterfly," he said, offering a hand. "Are you ready, Lila?"

She swallowed and then followed. "Yes. I think so. James?" she asked, tentative. "Why haven't you talked to my father?"

He sighed, squeezing her hand. "Just a matter of timing, Butterfly, that's all. I will soon. I would rather you were a year older, but this summer. Is that soon enough?" He paused to look at her.

She searched his face, but didn't see any lie in it. "All right. Summer." She would finish another year of school; that should be fine. A little spring came to her step. "Race?" she asked.

He chuckled. "I'm it?" he asked, raising a brow. "You didn't like it the last time I caught you."

She giggled. "Things change." She tore off through the grass, lifting her skirt.

James' loud laugh followed her, and then he caught up, running alongside. He tackled her to the ground, rolling over her. "All mine," he said, his face serious. "I will be talking to your parents, Lila. Don't doubt that. You will be mine forever."

Her stomach fluttered, all fear from before erased. He wouldn't simply take her and leave her. He needed her.

Holding his cheeks, she pulled him for a kiss. His hands moved from the grass, one holding her wrist gently, the other sliding up her leg, pulling it to his hip.

"We were interrupted earlier," he said, eyes fiery even in the moonlight.

Lila bit her lip. "I wasn't sad about that."

He paused in the middle of stroking her thigh. "Why is that, Butterfly?"

"We're not married," she said simply. "My mother..." She didn't really want to think about her mother.

"Yet, Lila. We aren't married yet. We are going to be. Would you like me to make my vows to you now? I will. I, James," he kissed her throat, easing himself down between her legs, "take you, Lila, to be my wife." His fingers brushed her skin, up over her pubic bone and along her belly, making her sigh. "To have, and to hold," he squeezed her bum and she giggled, "to love and to cherish," he kissed her lips briefly, "in sickness and in health," she heard his belt and felt him hot against her thigh. Her breath caught. "Until death do us part." He pushed into her, and she screamed.

It had hurt the first time he put his fingers in her, too, but not like this. She felt like she was being torn open, stretched and pulled. It burned and stung. After the first full scream, she whimpered with the pain.

"Shhh, Lila. Oh, I didn't mean for it to hurt, not this time. Lila?" James voice made it through the searing pain. That receded, to her delight, leaving her with a dull throb in its place. James was still perched over her, the hand not on her wrist wiping away tears.

She took a deep breath, pushing the pain away. It was a trick she had learned, a way of putting what bothered her into a corner of her mind, to be dealt with later. "Yours," she said softly.

He exhaled and half collapsed on her. He scooped her into his lap. "Mine," he said, brushing fingers through her hair. "All mine. Now and forever."

She smiled against his chest.

"It won't hurt as much next time," he said. Her eyes opened wide, filling with tears. Next time?

***

"Patricia? Is that you?"

Patty laughed, still buzzing in her high. She didn't really recognize her brother, but he had managed to identify her.

84

"What are you doing? Why are you with these men?" His eye went to the two who each held her by an arm.

"She's ours tonight, pal. Why don't you go find another? I hear Bruce has plenty," the man on her left said. "Buy them a line of coke, and they're yours for the night. Isn't that right, Patty?" His finger traced her jaw and she opened her mouth to bite it playfully. She missed, her vision not quite keeping up with the motion or her brain.

"Yeah, they've taken care of me, now I take care of them. Go on, Stuart, go home." She gave him a playful shove, stumbling and feeling her hips and ass grabbed by the men as they caught her.

"Tomorrow. I'm coming back, Patricia, and I'm taking you home." His voice was hard and didn't fit at all with the delightful lights and colors she was watching.

"Tomorrow. Sure. You buy me tomorrow. I'll take care of you too, Stewie." Too late she remembered he hated the nickname.

"Keeping it in the family, Patty? You are a raunchy thing." The other man spun her around and put his mouth on hers, his tongue sliding around her own. She relaxed a little into his hold, grateful she didn't have to keep her balance. Her tongue explored his mouth, too, awful tasting, like chewing tobacco. She couldn't care though, he was kissing her and that didn't hurt. It was likely something tonight would, but it was equally likely she'd still be too high to really feel it until morning. Then everything would hurt and it wouldn't matter either.

She didn't notice Stuart leave. She only half noticed her clothing being removed. Once the garments were gone, she was expected to perform, even in her dazed state. The men didn't seem disappointed, taking their turns with her.

She was startled when she woke to a punch to the face.

"Fuck, what?" she asked, holding her jaw. Bruce almost never hit her in the face. Back, legs and arms all the time, but the johns didn't want a walker with a shiner.

"Your brother came last night. Made a lot of trouble for me. Too much. More than your worth, Patty. I want you out. Now." His face was contorted in anger.

Her head was still in a fog. By the light in the window, she couldn't have been asleep more than a couple hours. She looked around, hoping this was some really bad dream and one of the other girls would wake her up.

"Now!" he shouted, kicking her in side.

Screaming, she curled around it. The other girls just watched, staying where they were. Half didn't even wake up.

"Fine," she groaned, tears still leaking. She grabbed her one change of clothes, but he knocked it from her hands.

"Those will go to Debbie. I bought them; they're mine. Be grateful I don't make you give me what you're wearing." Bruce's voice was as cold and hard as he was, a boulder of a man. No john messed with him, and the girls knew to have supple backbones, bend or break. They bent.

She wanted to spit at him, she wanted to scream and punch. That would only get her more bruises and probably broken bones. She stood, slowly, holding her side, and walked out. When she was on the street, she headed for a park, somewhere she could sit. She leaned against a tree and tried to figure out what had just happened. At least it was late spring. She would be freezing otherwise.

Bruce had said something about her brother. What brother? She did have four, but what brother would have come here? Slowly, pieces of the night before came back. Groaning at the stiffness in her side, she rose again. Stuart was going to have to make this up to her. Life out here was bad, but it was better than Fort Garland. She needed a new pimp, a new hit. She started looking for a ride to hitch.

Chapter Nine

George drove with purpose. He was missing out on the prime construction season, but he knew it wasn't futile this time. Nancy had actually told Eva today where James was.

After tracking down three of the sisters without any trace of James, Eva had shared something she'd previously thought irrelevant with George. When Nancy and Josh had first moved to Fort Garland, Eva's mother had invited Nancy over for tea. Eva had disliked her even then. Nearly twenty years later, and never a friendship between them, it had seemed a small and insignificant detail. As the search dragged on, however, she suggested she might be able to convince Nancy to come over for tea, and learn surreptitiously what they struggled to find on their own.

There had been several such afternoons, two month's worth. Eva hated having the vile woman over. She spent the night after such a tea complaining about how overbearing and prideful the woman was.

"Nothing is good enough for her. No wonder Joshua spends as little time at home as possible."

In the end, Nancy had told them what they needed. James was staying with her sister in Knoxville. It took restraint not to speed. George had a name; he'd look up the address when he arrived.

Then, he would let passion dictate what came next. He'd had images of himself with weapons, knives most often, giving James scars to match Daphne's. Sometimes he just used his fists in the dreams. Always, he left with James' blood on his hands and a smile on his face.

He had a pocket knife; a simple thing he used more often as a screwdriver than not, but it had a blade.

He stopped for gas on the edge of town, planning to hit the phone booth to find the address.

"George?" someone called from the door to the store.

George's brow creased. He didn't know anyone in Knoxville. They must have been referring to someone else. He finished filling his tank and hung up the nozzle. That was when he saw Ron waving a three-fingered hand.

"Ron," he said with a smile, extending his hand to the trucker. "How are you?"

"Good. Thought I recognized you. Taking some ease for a spell. Had enough driving across country for a little while."

"You live here?" George asked, wondering if the world could really be so small.

"Sure do. What brings you here? Was Mae able to help you out?"

George frowned slightly. "Yes and no. She helped plenty. Sadly, what I was looking for wasn't in Kingman."

Ron crossed his arms. "It's here?" he asked, flatly. "Seemed you were looking for something less than savory. I don't know as I like it being in my hometown. I might have to help you root it out."

George smiled a little. "I might take you up on that. For the moment, do you know where Florence Greene lives?"

"Flo? Sure do. Has a tidy little farm on the north side. Surely she doesn't have anything to do with it. It's a toss-up between her and Matilda Everett which will take the most blue ribbons at the fair each year. I swear if those two women could get their noses any higher in the air, they'd fall flat on their rumps." Ron guffawed at his own joke.

"Sounds like her sister," George muttered.

Ron scratched his head with two fingers. "You know, Flo wouldn't be at home now. It's tea at the Everett's. Everyone who's anyone is over there. Obviously, I'm not anyone," he joked, nudging George with a shoulder.

George smiled back at him. He could snoop around the farm when no one was there. "Thanks, Ron. Really. I appreciate it." He tried to pry himself away, politely. Ron wasn't finished yet, though.

"You never did say what you were looking for. Something to do with your daughters?" Ron's brow creased.

George couldn't answer that, not really. "Yeah. A friend of hers."

"Good friend to have you scouring the country for her." Ron's brows rose this time, obviously not believing George.

"Yes," George replied. He'd appreciated all of Ron's help, but couldn't tell him anything more.

"You let me know if you need any more help, okay, George?" The way he said help made George think Ron knew more than he was letting on.

"I will, Ron. Where can I find you?"

"Oh, I live just up Maple, here. Number sixty-five." Ron smiled wanly, his eyes entreating George to tell him more.

"Sixty-five. Got it. Thanks." With that, he opened the door to the store and paid for his gas. When he came out, Ron was gone.

George's sigh was a mixture of relief and remorse. Ron would probably be a good person to have at his side, but he couldn't share what had happened to Daphne, with him or anyone. He parked his truck in a field access and walked to the farmstead, expecting it to be deserted.

He was in luck. There were no people around, just a lazy old hound who barely looked up at him, enjoying the shade under the porch too much to investigate. George skipped the main house; he didn't want to break and enter if he could help it. Instead he snooped in the out buildings, thinking maybe James was occupying one of them.

The smokehouse seemed to have been converted. It had a piece of foam thrown over a table for a bed, but no water, no electricity. He poked inside and sniffed in disdain. This room had been used — for sex. He felt his blood rise.

James hadn't been idle. He'd found another girl. George gripped the knob until pain shot up his hand. He pulled the knob hard and the hinges let go of rotting wood. He snarled, dropping the door beside him. He picked up the filthy cloth covering the foam and tore it in his hands. He felt threads cutting into his skin, but he didn't stop. After that he tossed the foam out the open doorway and put his foot through the table.

That was stupid, he thought to himself as his foot throbbed. He might have broken his foot, it hurt so badly. He was leaning on a tall cupboard and opened it. There were a couple changes of clothes, a girl's coat and boots. George ground his teeth, but closed that door, stomping out until his foot reminded him he should tread lightly.

He climbed the back steps, but that was when the hound decided that he didn't like this stranger. Wandering the outbuildings was fine, apparently, as long as George stayed away from the house.

Seeing the dog bearing teeth, George decided he didn't need a rabies shots on top of a possible cast and made his way back to his truck. He didn't need to see inside the house anyway. He knew where James was.

He paused at a young couple walking hand-in-hand. She was young with curly red hair, probably only sixteen. He had to be twenty with blond hair. "Excuse me," he asked, leaning out the window. "Can you direct me to the Everett's?"

The girl's eyes went a little wide, but the man answered, "Certainly. It's at the top of the hill, there. Big white one, number six."

"Thank you," George answered, driving on. He looked in his rear-view mirror to see the two arguing. The young man was tugging on the girl's arm. She resisted but was eventually swayed, dragging her feet slightly.

George put them out of his mind, climbing the hill. He parked on the street, the ample drive already filled with other vehicles. He heard chatting through the gate and knocked on it, pulling off his ball cap.

"Hello?" a woman with red hair pulled into an elaborate coif asked, peering at him with blue eyes. "Can I help you?"

"Possibly. I'm looking for Florence Greene, Ma'am. I was given to believe she would be here today."

The woman's sharp features made her sneer even more sinister. "You were correctly informed. Please, mister?"

"Kingston, Ma'am. I don't want to intrude," he said as she held the gate open to him. He was decidedly under-dressed in a plaid work shirt and jeans.

"Not at all. Any friend of Florence is welcome here." She smiled, showing perfect white teeth, and it was anything but friendly.

Another woman, this with blond hair flowing down her back in a loose braid stood, her pale pink dress smoothing around her. "What is this, Matilda?"

"Mister Kingston says he was told he could find you here. I presumed he was a friend of yours." The redhead's sneering smile turned to Florence. "Was I wrong?"

"Very," Florence answered. "I have never met this man before in my life."

George felt out of place. There were few men at the gathering, mostly boys. One of the older of these came over.

"Excuse me, sir. Would you like to join us?" he asked.

"Jeremy!" another woman called. "Be seated." she ordered. She was most likely Jeremy's mother.

George appreciated the effort. None of the boys here were old enough to be James, at any rate, so George opted to beat a retreat.

"If you ladies will excuse me. I'd actually come looking for Mrs. Greene's nephew, but I see he isn't here. I'll be on my way. Ma'am, Ma'am." He nodded to each of the women in turn, feeling decidedly inferior in their presence. It was only after the gate shut behind him that he wondered why that should be. Just because he wasn't dressed as well as they were didn't make him any less. In his mind, he chalked it up to being uninvited. He wasn't a welcome guest, that was all. Nothing to do with him in particular. He knew he was lying to himself.

Starting up the old Ford, he trundled back to the Greene farm, hoping to find some trace of James.

He was unlucky. He had no sooner parked than he saw a Lincoln Continental pass with Florence Greene at the wheel. He thought better of trying to confront her again, and turned back to town. He was parked outside the gas station, boots on the seat, leaning on the door. What to do next, he wondered.

There was a rap on his window.

"Hungry?" Ron asked, his voice coming over the top of the glass where it had been rolled down to give George any breeze available.

George chuckled. "You know it. You cook?"

Ron quirked an eyebrow. "With how often I'm home? Why would I bother to learn? My sister's always got enough for one more. And since she'll be expecting me, you can be the extra mouth tonight."

George didn't know what he had done to earn the man's grace, but he was glad for it. He hopped out of the truck, locking it, and followed Ron.

"Unca Ron!" a voice called, just before a toddler latched onto Ron's knees. The girl couldn't have been more than four.

"Yes, Izzy. You saw me yesterday, and the day before. Let an old man through!" He tried to walk with her still attached to one leg.

She giggled madly, hugging tighter.

"Grace! Get this leech off me," he bellowed as he passed through the front door.

"She isn't a leech. You'd have to have blood in that cold heart for her to suck out," a woman replied. George couldn't see her around Ron, but when the big man turned he saw someone that couldn't be less like the burly trucker if she tried. If anything, she reminded him of Mae with the same dark hair, long and straight, hanging to her waist in a simple tail. Where Ron was round and large, his sister was petite and wiry, probably no more than five feet. Her blue eyes found his quick enough when she rounded the corner.

"Well, hello," she said. "Izzy, get off your uncle's leg. Go wash your face and hands." She pried the child off Ron, gave each pigtail a tug, tightening the elastics holding them, and swatted her bottom gently. The child giggled and ran from the room. "I'm Grace, in case this sack of suet didn't have the sense to give you my name." Her voice drawled like Ron's, pulling the words like warm candy. Her hand was out-stretched and George started, putting his into her own.

"George," he said, shaking it. She gripped his a little harder and he returned it, feeling more at ease. "George Kingston. Just stopped in town for a day or two and Ron, here, invited me over. I can find a restaurant if-"

"Of course he did," Grace said, rolling her eyes. "Well, he's right." Her hips swayed slightly as she pushed by them out the door. George nearly jumped out of her way while Ron moved to give her a swat.

A spatula George hadn't seen in her hand came out to smack Ron on the wrist. He shook his hand, wincing. Only then did George notice the arsenal in her apron pockets. She also sported tongs, a wooden spoon, a baster and a brush of some sort.

"I have told you, big brother, you keep your hands to yourself." She turned again and George stood on the veranda to watch as she opened a grill and turned pieces of meat and foil wrapped potatoes. Her voice was loud and shrill as she called, "Chucky! Kenny! Supper is on!"

It was only moments, but a ruckus of snapping twigs and kicked rocks preceded a pair of boys, preteen, both covered in dirt. "Thanks, Ma," each said as they kissed her cheek.

"Don't forget to wake Pa," she called after them, loading all of the cooked food onto a platter that took both her arms to carry.

"Let me get the door for you," George offered as she squeezed by him.

"Why thank you, George. Don't worry about Ron inviting you. As he probably told you, I always have extras. Nicolas! Where did you come from?" she asked a boy of five or so who sat next to Izzy at the table. "Well, you might as well stay. Let me call your mother." Grace picked up the phone and dialed without looking. "As you can see, extra mouths aren't uncommon. Grab him a plate, Ron. I don't set the table anymore. I never know how many to seat! Hello? Mary? It's Grace ..."

George's brain was still flying with all the activity in the room, and his attention was taken from the phone call by the man who had to be Ron's brother-in-law. He stood well over six feet with light brown hair and eyes. He held a hand to George.

"Mark," he said. "George, was it? Nice to meet you. Sit over here, other side of Izzy. That way Ron can actually eat something."

Izzy smiled up at George as he moved to sit. One of the boys thumped a plate with cutlery on it in front of him.

"Hi," Izzy said, peeling foil from her potato quickly. "Will you cut it? It's too hot."

George smiled, remembering cutting food for his girls, and quickly ran his knife through the potato's skin, opening the white steamy flesh to the air. "Do you need me to cut your pork chop, too?" he asked, spearing one with a fork before the boys took off with it to the other end of the table.

"Yes, please," Izzy said, smiling up at him with perfect baby teeth. "Are you an uncle?" she asked.

George laughed, working the pork chop into small cubes. "No, just a friend. I won't be here long. Probably not even tomorrow night."

Her face fell. "Oh. Nick, can I have your beans? I'll give you carrots." The two started swapping vegetables and George was forgotten.

He sighed a little as he ate, missing his family, but feeling closer to them at the same time. It didn't go unnoticed.

"Anything the matter, George?" Grace asked, wiping Izzy and Nick's faces before they ran off to play. The boys were already gone.

"Not really. Missing the girls."

Her eyebrow raised a little. Ron chuckled and elbowed her. "He has three daughters. Mind on the table, Gracie."

"Well, with you traveling men, one never knows," she rolled her eyes. "You'll excuse me, George. I simply assume if he knows you," she stuck a thumb at Ron, "that you must be another trucker."

"No, actually. I work in construction." Grace rose and filled glasses with iced tea. She doled a shot or rum into each one before serving them.

"What brings you to Knoxville then?" she asked, setting a perspiring glass in front of George, Mark and Ron before retaking her seat. "You just passing through?"

George hung his head a little. He really hated not being able to tell these people. "I'm looking for James Spencer," he said, as upfront as he could be. Ron nodded a little, encouraging him to continue. "He ... he wronged my family, and I came seeking justice."

Grace's eyebrows rose. "Justice?" she asked. "You seek it, or you're delivering it? You look like you didn't come to report him." She sipped her tea, her blue eyes holding his fast. She seemed to see right through him. When he managed to break her gaze, it was picked up by Ron, who still had a twinkle in his.

Thinking back to his sessions with Wanda, he knew this was something he sought for himself. Was there anything wrong with him wanting vengeance? He met Grace's eye again. She didn't seem to be holding his reason for coming against him, just curious and watching his responses. She was Ron's opposite in every way. While Ron merely looked eager to help him out, Grace was appraising. She was willing to help but not eager, willing to talk him out if that's what he needed. What did he need?

"I'm not sure. Perhaps not justice."

Grace's lips twitched, her nose crinkling a bit with her smile. "Need a night to sleep on it? Ron has a spare room."

"Offering up my house, woman?"

"Of course I am! I'm the one that cleans it when you're gone a month at a time!" her voice was as loud as his and held more indignation. "If you're going to have a second bed, the least you can do is have someone sleep in it once in a while."

Ron's head hung slightly. "You know why I have a double bed," he said softly. Grace's expression softened as well and she patted his arm.

"I do. Now let George have it the night so he's not stuck sleeping in his truck."

"I never said I wouldn't."

"Well then be less of a bear!"

"Are they always like this?" George asked Mark.

He didn't answer, except to nod. George thought that with the noise in this house, he could understand why Mark might be soft-spoken.

He followed Ron home. "The bed is for the girls," George surmised as Ron opened the unlocked door.

"Yep. If their mother ever deemed me worthy to see them for more than an hour, I thought they should have a room of their own. It's the only room in here that looks like anything."

George stepped through the doorway and immediately understood. The walls were practically bare. One photograph, of Ron with his wife and girls, hung over a cold fireplace that probably hadn't had a fire in it in decades. Another, of Grace and her family, sat on the mantle. There was no relief, and no rhyme to the place. The couch was brown corduroy, but the curtains were blue and walls yellow. The rug on the wooden floor, a hooked affair, had probably been handmade by someone, not Grace though. There was nothing else in the main room, no television, no radio.

"Follow me," Ron said, opening a door. George noticed Ron hadn't taken off his shoes, but he doffed his boots. The floor looked clean, and he didn't want to dirty it.

Tugging off his boot, he winced. It hadn't bothered him much through dinner, though now that he thought of it, he hadn't taken his boots off there. Grace must think him an uncivilized lout. The thought was lost in the throb that came from his swollen foot as he took a step. Ron saw him wince.

"Something wrong?" He looked at George's stocking feet. "You don't have to take off your shoes," he said. "I never do."

George didn't want to think about trying to wedge his boot back on now. He stepped lightly, hobbling a little, until he was behind Ron. "Think I sprained something."

Ron opened the door and George bit back a snort.

"It's the girls' room," Ron said in a growl. George made a note never to get on Ron's bad side.

97

"I know, but ..." He paused, trying to phrase this properly. "I'm not sure I'll be able to sleep in there." He bit off a chuckle.

Ron took another look in the room and George squeezed past him to make the point.

The room was pink. A pink cover on the bed and pink curtains on the window gave the room a rosy glow. Stuffed animals of varying sizes sat on the bed and a collection of dolls on a shelf. There was a doll house in the corner and a pink rug on the wooden floor, the same floor from the living room. In the middle of it stood George, in blue and green plaid shirt and worn, faded blue jeans, with stubble on his chin and sun weathered skin. He grinned at Ron, hands in his pockets.

The old trucker doubled up laughing. "You look ridiculous in here!" he roared. "You look like a pig in a cowherd." He continued laughing.

George took another look around; it'd be fine after the sunset, if the stuffed animals were out of the way. "Judging by the colors, I'd say I'm the cow in the pigsty, but..."

"It's not a pigsty," Ron growled, humor gone.

"I meant pink pigs. Ease up, man. I'm sure your girls would love it. I kinda like it myself," he pondered, scratching his chin. He needed to shave. "Get in touch with my feminine side." It was some of the feminist bullshit he tried not to pay attention to, but it had the desired effect.

Ron slapped his knee, barking another laugh. "No touching yourself in their room!" He laughed as he said it, knowing George planned no such thing. "God, you're a good'un, George. Come on out; I'll get ya a cold one."

George chuckled and limped to the kitchen. It seemed to have a little more coordination to the colors; dark yellow curtains, green cabinets, same brown wooden floor. The dining set matched the floor, almost disappearing into it.

Ron cracked open two bottles, letting the caps fall to the floor. George scooped them up and tossed them in the can before taking his bottle.

"Thanks," Ron muttered, lighting a cigarette. "I'm too used to drinking in bars." He took a long swallow followed by a short drag. "So what did you do to your foot?"

George grimaced and sat heavily in one of the chairs, crossing his leg for a better look. "Put it through a table?" he admitted as a question, asking if Ron believed him.

He snorted and shook his head, smoke circling him. "Lucky if you didn't break it then. Bad table?"

"Evil," George said, his voice cold as he remembered what James had most likely done on that table with another girl as innocent as Daphne.

Ron gaped for a moment, then stepped forward, putting his bottle on the table and holding his cigarette in his lips. He put both hands on George's foot. George winced, but otherwise held still. The odd shape of his two fingers and thumb distracted from the pain as Ron manipulated the bones.

"Not broken or you'd be screaming to high heaven. Probably a sprain, like you said. I'd put ice on it, if I was you." Leaving his bottle on the table and taking the smoke from his mouth, he turned to the fridge. Opening the freezer, he pulled out a handful of cubes and stuck his smoke back in his mouth to grab a towel. He handed the makeshift ice pack to George.

After pulling off his sock, George set his foot on the cubes, sucking in breath, then tied the towel over the top. He grabbed for his beer again, still breathing sharply.

"Thanks," he said raising the bottle to Ron, who lifted his in return, taking it from the table again.

***

George cracked his eyes in the pink haze, trying to figure out where he was. He'd had James on his knees, about to begin his retribution when the light intruded. It had been much better than the dreams of Daphne on the table in that smokehouse. He grimaced, blinking to rid himself of that memory.

Grace stood in the doorway, hands on hips. "You aren't going to find anyone lying there," she said, tapping a toe.

George realized he was lying in his underwear, the pink cover tossed to the floor. He sat up and grabbed for it, but not before noticing Grace rolling her eyes.

"Please, George, I have two boys, three if you count Ron. Nothing I haven't seen before. Except maybe that foot. Let me see that." She came and sat at the far end of the bed, taking George's still swollen right foot in her hand. "You did a good job on this. Kick a wall?"

"A table," he croaked.

"Grace! Are you in my house?!" Ron bellowed.

"No! Go back to bed, you lazy buffoon!" she shouted back, barely looking up from George's foot.

"Ron said nothing's broken," George told her, propping himself up a little.

"He did? Well, he's probably right, there. You should stay off it for the day, but you won't," she finished with a sigh, setting it on the bed. "You have something you need to be doing. James Spencer. He's staying at the Greene farm?" Grace asked, though George could see she already knew.

"Yes. How did you-?"

"Ah." She raised a finger, stopping him. "And you went looking for him at the Everett's?" she asked, her brows rising.

George hung his head sheepishly. He did not want to repeat that experience.

"Well, now you know why I'm not eager to head to the Greene farm," he grumbled, grabbing his shirt off the floor and pulling it on. It was already warm enough that he almost wished he could leave it off. He shoved his legs through his jeans, pulling his foot from her lap.

"Indeed," she answered, smirking. "How would you like to know where James Spencer works, instead?" She held her chin in one hand, regarding him coolly.

George blinked, falling back to his ass on the bed and jostling Grace slightly. "You know where he works?"

Grace smiled. "I do. Still want to rush out the door?"

George shook his head.

"Good, I'm getting you something to eat first. Assuming Ron keeps anything in his fridge." She pushed up and strode for the kitchen, George on her heels.

After toast and coffee, all Grace was able to find in Ron's kitchen, George looked at his boots and grimaced. Grace had told him where James was working, the Ford lot, before leaving. Apparently, James' uncle owned the dealership. It wasn't far away; normally George would just walk there. He continued to look at his boots.

"I have some sandals," Ron said.

George looked up, smiling. "Thank you," he said. The straps were easily loosened to accommodate his swollen foot. It turned out Ron's feet left enough room that George's could slip in easily. He tightened the other. Testing his weight, he smiled back at his new friend. "I really don't know how to thank you and Grace." They had both done so much for him and they still only had a vague notion why. "My daughter would thank you," he said, choking a little.

"Now, now, I'll have to trade you rooms if you get all soft. It's the pink, I'm sure of it," Ron teased, trying to give George an avenue of retreat.

He took it, smiling. "Maybe. I'm sure I've lost machismo just from exposure."

Ron guffawed. "Well, perhaps you'll be on your way home tonight."

George smiled, filled with hope. "Perhaps."

Ron gave him one last clap on the shoulder before turning to the kitchen.

George watched the car lot from his truck. He saw three different salesmen, two younger with blond hair. He didn't know which one was James. Both wore white shirts and black ties. Both smiled at the older man, Victor Greene most likely. Both tried to make a sale. He couldn't know if they succeeded, not from here.

Grumbling, he waited until the end of the day, hoping James would be riding home with Greene. His luck was terrible. All three men got into the same Lincoln Continental George had seen Florence driving the day before.

He turned his ignition in disgust and peeled off for the farm, trying to reach it ahead of them. James would be the one staying at the house. He realized that he didn't know if the Greene's had a son of their own.

Slapping his steering wheel in anger, he yanked the parking brake and jumped out. The pain in his foot brought him out of the fog of rage quickly. Thinking more clearly, he walked toward the farmyard. He needed to be near enough to see when Greene got home.

He saw movement in the back, in the smokehouse. Frowning, George changed direction. It couldn't be James, unless they knew a faster way here, and even then, the car wasn't parked in the drive.

He saw a flash of red through the window and then a girl came out of the small wooden hut. Her skin was pale, her nose freckled. Her eyes widened when she saw him and she started to run.

"Wait!" he called, knowing he couldn't chase her with a banged up foot. Damn, she was fast. He watched her streak away. He recognized her though, and suddenly he knew which blond man was James. He had asked that pair for directions to the Everett house. Who was she, though?

He hobbled back to his truck. Now that he knew who James was, he could plan his confrontation. He didn't want the Greenes involved, if possible. If he could interrupt another meeting in that ... hole so much the better. He looked into the smokehouse, not surprised to see the foam back, on the ground now, and a new sheet placed over it. He doubted a better opportunity would present itself, so he closed the door behind himself and sat on the mat, waiting.

He couldn't be sure of the time, but it had seemed hours since sunset. George figured if the couple was coming, they would have been here by now. He stretched, hands pressing the top of the tiny building and stepped out, walking back to where he left his truck.

Rather than risk waking Ron, he slept in his car. He was woken by the sun on the horizon. Looking down the road, he saw that the Lincoln was still in the drive at the Greene farm. He needed a better plan, and he wanted to know who that red-haired girl was. He drove to Grace's house. She knew everything else, after all.

George knocked on the screen door as he opened it. Grace was watching Izzy as she cut paper with a pair of scissors. She looked up as he walked in.

"George! We thought you'd left. Doubly so when I heard ... oh dear," she ended quietly. "George, I'm afraid I have bad news."

"He's gone," George surmised, thumping into one of the chairs. He watched Izzy make a chain of dolls. She smiled at him.

"Apparently he left in the night. But if it wasn't you ..." Grace's eyes wandered the kitchen. "Penny," she said suddenly, darting for the phone. "I asked her about James. She must have said something to Flo. Oh, I'm sorry, George," she frowned as she listened to the other end of the line. "Hello, Penny? It's Grace. No, I hadn't heard that. Is that right?" Grace smiled and shrugged, continuing in her role as part of the gossip chain.

"What?!" she said suddenly. "He's gone? I didn't know. Where has he gone? Does anyone know? I see. You did hear about the Johnson girl, didn't you?" She winked at George. He tried not scowl, instead taking the scissors and making a cutout of his own.

He stretched out the string, hand to hand, toe to toe. Izzy giggled. George smiled, too.

Grace finally rejoined them. "Sorry about that. No word has reached her about where James has gone. Short of asking Flo herself, I don't have a way of knowing. I wouldn't wager on her telling me if she did know. We aren't exactly in the same circle."

George nodded. "He has a girl, James does. A red-head, about sixteen?" He didn't have a lot of information to give Grace.

She frowned in thought. "Curly hair? Or straight?" she asked.

"Curly, ringlets, like fire." He remembered watching them bounce as she ran. "And fast. She's a runner."

Grace smiled. "I'll bet that's Lila Everett. Matilda hates it when she runs, but that girl could race the wind. I don't remember anyone mentioning anything, though. That pair would be remarked in all the circles," she mused tapping her lip with a forefinger. "It's secret?" she verified.

George nodded. "Most likely. Daphne..." he cut off. "It wasn't until after James had left town that I knew anything. My daughter kept it that quiet."

Grace's jaw slackened slightly. "He ... Do you think Lila has ...? Oh, Matilda will flip her lid when she finds out." Grace put her hand to her mouth now. "Poor, Lila. I wonder if she even knows he left?"

George shrugged. "I don't think so. She came by the Greene farm while I was there, probably expecting to find him."

Izzy looked from her mother to George. "What are you talking about?"

"Why don't you go outside and play for while, Izzy? Maybe Nick or Lucy are out there." She patted the girl's shoulder, urging her of her chair.

Izzy sighed loudly but complied. Grace's eyes never really left George. They were filled with concern. "You need sleep," she said in the end. "Head over to Ron's and kick him out of his bed. His room is always dark, tinfoil," she scoffed. "He'll be up by now anyway. Go on. I'll see if I can learn anything more for you."

George just looked at her for a moment. "You and Ron are too good, Grace. I just show up on your step-"

"Nonsense," she cut him off. "If Matilda Everett's daughter has been having a relationship behind her mother's back ... Well, I'll be the queen bee of the rumor mill for a while!" She smiled cruelly. "Matilda needs to be dropped a peg a six," she muttered. "So don't worry about this being any trouble for me, it's just something I do, luckily for you."

"Lucky me," he echoed, pushing himself out of the chair. "Thank you so much."

"Don't worry about it!" she said, shooing him. "Just be back here at six for supper." She made that an order rather than an invitation.

George couldn't help but smile.

Waking at five, he found Ron downstairs and mentioned slipping out to call his family. Ron encouraged him to use the phone, despite George's arguments to the contrary.

Marlene answered. "Hello?"

"Hey, Muffet. Is Mom busy?" he asked.

"Um, yeah, kinda. She's at the stove. Are you coming home soon?" she asked, hopeful.

"Soon, yes. I should be home for the weekend," he said, rubbing his face. Unless he was headed somewhere else, he thought to himself.

"Good! There's a party at the lake this weekend, and I was hoping I could take out the boat. There'll be..."

"Wait, wait. I can't be positive I'll be back, and that boat needs repairs, Muffet. Besides, I'm not sure I want you taking one out yourself yet." Although he still felt the pang of disappointment from coming so close to his goal, it was nice to deal with something mundane and familiar.

"Oh," she said, and he could hear her pout. "Maybe next time?" she said, brightening a little.

He chuckled. "Maybe next time, after I've gone out with you again once." He wasn't overly concerned, Marlene wasn't irresponsible, but he wanted to see her handle the motor since she'd gained the upper body strength to start it on her own, and how she responded to failures or malfunctions.

"Janet wants to talk," she said with a sigh, bringing George out of his plans.

His youngest daughter spoke brightly into the phone. "Hi, Daddy! I miss you!!"

"I miss you too, love. You keeping out of trouble?"

"I'm never in trouble," she lied. "Well, not big trouble." That was true. "I've learned how to double dutch! I only fell three times today!" She sounded thrilled. He had no idea what "double dutch" was, but thought it must be something done outside, as she talked about grass stains and dirt in her knees. Then ropes ... ah, skipping. He still wasn't positive, but he answered and praised at all the right intervals, hoping Eva would be finished supper soon.

"Oh, Mom's here," Janet said at last. George fought not to sigh.

"Hello, dear," she said, a touch tired herself. "What's the news?"

"Bad," he growled. "James left in the night. And he has another girl here!" he nearly shouted before he realized. His voice simply rose instead. "I don't know what I'm going to do now," he said, holding his head again.

"You're going to learn what you can and come home," she said calmly.

"He's going to do this again," he said quietly. "Wherever he has gone, he'll find another girl. I can't let him, Eva. I can't." His voice rose again and he noticed his hand shaking.

"Then you'll stop him. We can tell people, George. Daphne is doing so much better these days. She's telling me more. It'll be hard for her, but if she knows it will help someone else, I don't think she'll balk at doing it, do you?"

George rubbed his eyes. He wanted to prevent his daughter reliving that any more than necessary, but if he couldn't uncover where James had gone, he didn't see any other choice.

"No," he finally answered, sighing. "No, she won't. She already told me she wouldn't. She shouldn't have to, Ev!" he shouted again. "It isn't fair!" He realized he sounded like Janet and stopped.

"No, it isn't," Eva agreed. "It isn't fair that this happened to Daphne, and it isn't fair that it happened to that girl there. But we can make sure it doesn't happen to anyone else. If we had ..." she drifted off.

It might not have happened to Lila, George filled in. If they'd reported him right away, he might not have. George needed to punch something. He slammed his fist hard on the table, but it didn't help.

"George, calm down," Eva urged through the line. "What's done is done. We're going to work with what is."

He nodded, knowing she was right, but still shaking with rage. "I love you," he murmured.

"I love you, too," she answered. "Come home soon."

"Tell Daphne and the others that I love them, too."

"Of course, George. We all miss you."

"Good-bye," he croaked, hanging up. He walked out to his truck and punched the passenger door. There were enough dings that the new dent didn't really make much difference. His hand throbbed, though. For some reason, that did make him feel better.

George had his boots on when he walked with Ron to Grace's house. The swelling had gone down enough for him to squeeze it on without too much pain. Just as well if he was going to head home any time soon. Walking didn't hurt as much either, to his relief.

It was after dinner, roast beef tonight, that Grace gave him the news she had. "No one has any idea where he went. In fact, several of my friends told me Flo is nearly beside herself. Apparently, James left without telling her that he was going. Also ..." she paused, making sure all of the children were off and occupied. "Lila is late."

George's brow wrinkled. Ron and Mark looked as stumped. "Late for what?" he asked.

Grace rolled her eyes. "Men," she muttered. "Her cycle is late."

George's eyes went wide. "P-pregnant?" he stuttered.

"Not for certain. Apparently Matilda is in almost as bad a state as Flo. She keeps telling people that Lila's only just started her cycles. They can be rather erratic at first," she explained to the men. "So it might be nothing, but she's worried about it just the same. She's been swearing up and down that she'll disown the girl if she's done anything as foolish as getting knocked up."

George stared at the center of the table, not sure what to make of this information. "Disown ... She'd throw her out?" George asked in disbelief. Even if Daphne had actually chosen to be with James, he couldn't imagine throwing her out of his house.

Grace was nodding. "I believe it. Matilda Everett is a cold woman. That's part of the reason I never tried to make it into her circle." She shook her head now.

George found himself doing the same. "When would she know?" he asked, still finding himself out of his element. "The girl ... when would she know if she was pregnant."

Grace shrugged. "Without a test, she wouldn't know until the baby started kicking, if she continued to believe her period was just erratic. I'm guessing Matilda has her tested soon if only to settle her own mind, or stop the rumors." Grace added it as an afterthought, but her eyes told George that she believed that was the real reason.

George put his chin in his hand, looking over his new friends. "You don't mind me poking around here another day? I'm curious about this girl. I feel ... obligated to her. There must have been some way I could have prevented her falling in with James." They still didn't know everything, but they knew enough. Grace reached across the table to take and squeeze his hand.

"I'm sure you did the right thing, George," she said, consoling him. "It might be nothing, after all."

George shook his head. "Even if she isn't ... pregnant," he shuddered to think of it, "she was touched by that ..." He looked up. It was more than he had told them before. Mark's eyes were pitying. Ron's seemed to fill with rage. Grace just smiled with understanding.

"I thought you were just looking for a man who ran out on your girl. He ..." Ron rumbled beside him. "You're a damn sight calmer than I would be, that's all I'll say."

George smiled a little. "I've had a few months," he told Ron.

That night, George couldn't sleep. Maybe it was the dolls on the wall. Maybe it was the thought of Lila Everett. In any case, he slipped quietly out of Ron's house. He started up his truck, not sure where he was headed, just looking for something to distract him. He found himself taking the route he had a number of times already, one that ended at the Greene farm. He frowned, looking at it, the site of his defeat, the end of the trail. He slumped over his wheel, brooding. Once his eyes adjusted from the light of the headlights to the dark, he noticed a shadow moving in the outbuildings.

"No," he whispered, getting out and walking carefully through the black field. There was rustling, much more than an animal would make, and the cut off sound of sobs.

He shook his head and walked up to the smoke house. He could see her moving inside. It looked like she was packing, grabbing the few belongings James had left here.

George knocked once before opening the door, and still Lila nearly bowled him over. He caught her by the shoulders.

"You're not James," she said looking up at him. Her eyes were adjusted to the dark, too.

He could see the reflection of the moon, lighting the tears in her eyes. She wiped her cheeks with one hand and sniffled, clutching her sack closer, as though it would protect her.

"No, I most certainly am not," George said with disdain. "What are you doing here, Lila?"

"I might ask you the same thing," she said, drawing herself up and for a moment reminding him of her mother. She seemed to suddenly be looking down on him, even though she was several inches shorter.

"I'm not sure what I'm doing here. Waiting for you, I suppose. Or waiting for James?" He supposed that was what she was doing.

She trembled slightly in his hand. "Well, it could be a very long wait," she said. "Now, if you'll excuse me ..." She started to shove past him.

"Heading home?" he asked.

"Who are you?" she asked in return.

"You aren't, are you?" George noticed that the sack held more than the items from the cupboard here. She was running away, or she had been kicked out. In either case, she needed help. The more he looked at her, the more he felt he owed it to her.

"Who are you?" she asked again. The Greene's dog howled suddenly. "Never mind, I have to get out of here. A lift?" she asked, smiling slightly.

"Your chariot awaits," he joked, turning aside to let her pass.

Chapter Ten

"Lila. Take this with you into the bathroom please."

Lila looked at her mother in disbelief. It was a cup, a paper cup. "What am I supposed to do with this?"

"Fill it," her mother said, firm lipped. Her eyes made her intent clear.

Lila swallowed. Her mother may have waited until that first false blood to explain her period to her, but she understood there were two that hadn't come. She knew what it probably meant. A baby? Growing inside her? It couldn't really be possible, could it? It would certainly mark her James' more than anything else they had done. But what was the cup for?

She held the cup under her, red-faced as she had been a year ago when she'd first touched herself here, and gathered pee in the cup. She flushed the rest and took the cup to her mother, curious what she had planned for it.

She held some plastic thing Lila had never seen before. "You don't want to know what this cost me. They'll be cheaper soon, but ..." Her mother tossed her head. "Never mind that. It's better than some stupid frog eggs anyway. I can show this to people." She dipped one end into the cup, and then placed both in the sink.

"Now, you will tell me who he is." Her mother's blue eyes seemed grayer than normal, steely. Lila shivered.

"James," she said in a whisper. "James Sp-spencer," she stuttered out. "I told him to talk to you and father. I begged him ..." she tried to explain, but her mother had already turned back to the sink, tapping her finger to her lips.

"James Spencer. Does Florence know?" she didn't seem to be asking Lila who kept silent. "No. She would have said something, gloated." Lila watched her mother pace. When those gray-blue eyes found her again, she backed up. "If you've gotten yourself knocked up, girl, you will leave this house. Do you understand me? I don't care who he is. I won't have the Everett name besmirched because of you." Lila had not felt a lot of love at her mother's hand, but she'd never suffered such complete hostility. Always her reprimands had come with some concern for Lila's welfare, even it had taken Lila days to puzzle out how. This ... this was to protect her own welfare, her name, not Lila.

Lila's lips trembled when she realized just how little she was regarded by her mother. Her father, she knew, had never thought much of her. Always home late and gone early, what time he had was for Christian, her brother, not her. She'd accepted that. It seemed common among her classmates with brothers, a thing of fathers and sons.

Lila watched her mother make another slow circuit of the kitchen before peering into the sink.

"Start packing," her mother said coldly. "One bag only, please. No sense taking more than you can carry. And don't think of taking any of your pins and rings. Those are family heirlooms." The ice in her mother's voice froze her on the spot. She was given one more stare before her mother turned, headed for her own room. "Be out of here before your father gets home."

Lila burst into tears, running to her room. She didn't bother to look in the sink. It didn't matter what the contraption was or how her mother knew. She couldn't have stayed even if she weren't ...

pregnant. She stopped just inside her door as the thought really struck her. She crossed her arms over her middle. Pregnant.

She looked down at her abdomen and lifted her dress, looking at it over her panties. It was still flat, well, the same small pouch of fat had been there for years. There was a baby growing in there? It didn't seem possible.

The grandfather clock downstairs, chiming the half-hour, shook her from her thoughts. She needed to get out of here. Baby or no baby, her mother obviously had no love for her. Why should she stay? She'd go to James.

She stopped again, hands in her drawer, gripping undergarments. James was gone. He'd left her too. What was she going to do? How could she live? Where could she live?

"Get a hold of yourself," she said aloud. "Plenty of sixteen year-olds support themselves fine. Mother married when she was sixteen." She skipped right over the fact that she wasn't sixteen yet. She wiped her cheeks roughly and started shoving skirts, blouses and dresses in a sack after hose and underwear. It was over half-full, but she didn't want to bother with her finer things; they'd be unlikely to do her much good, not where she was going.

Where was she going?

Coats, boots, she hadn't packed these things. James kept spares. The shed. She could stay there. The Greene's wouldn't notice her, not right away. She could get her feet under her. She ran down the stairs now that she had a plan.

Christian was waiting for her.

"Is it true?" he asked. "Did you really ... Lila! I haven't even ..." Lila blushed scarlet, clutching her bag. "Well," he continued. "That's not why I'm here. Here." He held out a book to her. When she didn't take it, he shoved it in the top of her bag. "Photographs. Mostly of me, you and me. I don't hate you. I'll miss you." He looked up at her sadly. "I won't forget you, Lila." He hugged her tight for a moment, startling her. Christian had never been affectionate to her. More often chasing her, pulling her hair, pushing her into the mud. As he left, she realized that *was* affection, boy affection.

"I'll miss you, too," and as she said it, she knew it was true. "I love you." Then she pulled on shoes and ran out the door, hat held to her head.

The sun was setting as she ran through fields. The sack, with her hat now inside, was slung on her back. Once the bag was settled, she let her stride open, kicking her heels as she hadn't in months. Her blood thumped hard and strong, making her head swim. It was pure joy to feel her muscles work in unison, her breath coming to match her stride, not heavy, not quick, perfect. Her hair streamed behind her and she laughed.

She was free. It was strange that she should feel good about being cast off, but she did. She was free of her mother and her mother's rules. She was free of her place in society.

She was free of James. Saddened, she slowed. She didn't want that; she wanted him, wanted him to care for her. He had cared for her, hadn't he? Why hadn't he ever talked to her parents? Surely, if he had, this wouldn't have happened this way.

The sun had fully set by the time she walked up to the door of the former smokehouse. Her steps had dragged at the end, questioning the father of the baby that was growing inside her. She hugged herself again as the door closed.

"I will take care of us," she promised. "I can do that much. We'll be alright." She sniffed and realized she'd started crying again. She shook her head, feeling weary. She'd had no supper. That was probably it. She looked at the mat on the floor. She'd been there with him just once. He didn't say what had happened to the cot or table or whatever had held it up before. She laid down on it, still able to smell him, and her, she noticed. She curled into a ball, and wept again until she slept.

Waking in the pitch black frightened Lila. Her room always had a little light, from street or moon or hall, but it was truly dark here. She knew it, though. Relaxing quickly, she remembered that she had never slept here, that was all, never woken here. She got up and stretched. With careful steps, she picked her way around outside. James said they kept the fruit in one of these buildings. Her stomach rumbled, and she'd give almost anything for a peach or a pear. She found the store house and pulled out two of the new crop, finishing the first ripe peach before making it back to the smokehouse. She stood outside as she gobbled the second.

Was that a rustling? She could have sworn she heard something. It might have been Grover, the Greene's old basset hound. Still, better to be inside, she thought, opening the door. Possibly better to be gone. She didn't need any of the Greene boys finding her here. She started pulling her clothes from the cupboard. Memories threatened to overwhelm her, and she felt tears in her eyes but didn't stop pulling out her things.

One rap was all the warning she had before the door to the shed opened. Startled, she stuffed the coat she held into the bag and stood, clutching the bundle to herself.

The figure was definitely male. Was it James? Had he come back for her after all? She thought she might weep for joy and ran to him.

He caught her by the shoulders, holding her a little away from him. James wouldn't do that. He took every opportunity to hold her tightly.

"You're not James," she declared, certain, tilting her chin up to regard the strange man. He had a fuzziness to his jaw, a beard maybe? And his hair seemed dark. He was about the same height as James but broader. He smelled of wood and grease, definitely not like James.

Oddly, one of the hands holding her shoulders let go and wiped across her cheeks. The threatening tears had rolled at some point. She sniffed in disdain and held her pack up, hoping to hide a little.

"I most certainly am not." His voice was deeper than James' as well, though not harder. "What are you doing here, Lila?" He seemed to be accusing her.

She drew herself up as her mother had taught her, her posture perfect. Taking a deep breath to steady herself before she spoke, she tried to put authority in her voice. "I might ask you the same thing," she finally said, feeling scandalous as she did. Who was she? A runaway. A castoff.

The man took a moment to answer but actually seemed a little abashed. Had her show actually had an effect? She would eat her shoes if it had. "I'm not sure what I'm doing here," he said quietly.

As she thought on the question and the answer, it did seem a good one. Who would be on the Greene farm in the middle of the night? He wasn't one of the Greenes, she was sure. None of them smelled like ... work.

"Waiting for you, I suppose," he continued, in the same plodding manner. He sounded off, like he wasn't from here. "Or waiting for James?"

James. Her heart crumpled a little. He had left her, left her to face the future, their baby, alone. She thought she would cry again. No. Not in front of this stranger. He still held her, she realized, and drew herself up again.

"Well, it could be a very long wait," she spat, her disappointment heavy in her voice. "Now if you'll excuse me ..." she pushed forward, intent on escape. Escape from memories, from this place, from this man, whoever he was.

"Headed home?" he asked.

She froze in place. What did he know? The way he said that. He knew! He knew she'd been banished. Who was he?

"You aren't, are you?" She was sure she hadn't spoken aloud, but he continued to show impossible knowledge of her situation. She was a girl on her own; she couldn't afford to put her trust in some stranger.

"Who are you?" she asked. Then shaking herself, she said what she'd meant. "Never mind, I have to get out of here." Abruptly, it occurred to her that he likely didn't run here as she had. He would have a car. "A lift?" she asked. She didn't trust him, but her friends had told of hitched rides plenty of times. If he could get her out of this place, away from everyone who ever knew her, she'd have an easier time starting over.

He smiled and the moon reflected off his teeth. "Your chariot awaits," he said.

He was mocking her! She drew herself up once more, wondering if she'd have to learn to walk on her toes to maintain the pose. "Lead the way," she said, treating him like a servant. They had a couple, colored people who worked for her family. A cleaning woman, a gardener. The man chuckled, but held the door open for her and then led when she paused in the field.

He stopped in front of a beat-up looking truck. Well, it was a vehicle. It had brought him here; it could carry her away. She climbed into the passenger seat, setting her bag between them.

"Now, really," she said, dropping any pretensions. "Who are you?"

"My name is George," he said, starting the engine. The second gee was lost in the roar. The headlights blinded them both for a moment.

***

Lila woke in a pink room. Completely pink. She stared for a moment in shock. There were dolls on a shelf on one wall and stuffed animals beside her. She was actually clutching one of the bears and pushed it away.

It took a moment, but memory returned to her. George. His daughter had known James. This room belonged to a friend of his, his daughters. She pushed herself up and saw she'd been sleeping in her underwear. Grabbing the dress she had doffed in the night, she yanked it over her head before opening the door. She could make out three voices, one female, all adult. She tiptoed through the living room.

Two men sat at the table, while a woman filled coffee mugs. She was the youngest and prettiest of them. Black hair fell to the middle of her back. Of the two men, one was nearly bald and the hair he had was gray. He looked mean, rough, and he only had two fingers on his right hand! She gasped and put her hand to her mouth.

George, the other man, saw her then. "Lila! Are you all right? Did you get some sleep?" He rose and came to her touching her arm gently. She hadn't gotten a good look at him in the dark, but she recognized his voice. He was tall, just short of six feet, with liberal gray in his dark hair. His eyes were such a warm brown that they made Lila melt a little. They were filled with concern for her, something she wasn't used to.

She felt the prickling in her eyes, tears. Hadn't she cried enough yet?

"Give her a little space, George," the woman said. "I'm Grace, Lila. This oaf is my brother, Ron."

"Hi," the man said, waving his two fingers and thumb. Lila shuddered slightly.

"Lila?" George asked, bringing her attention back to him. He had told her so little last night. Something about his daughter and James. "Are you alright, Lila?"

"Yes," she said. "I'm fine." She stepped past him to the table where several pieces of toast rested on a plate. Sitting, she helped herself to one, munching hungrily.

"Good." His voice was filled with relief. He sat down across from her, watching.

"Well, if you've no more need of me, I should get back to Izzy. Nita won't appreciate me leaving her there too long, though she keeps Ian out of trouble. I live right across the road, Lila, in case you need a woman's help," she said gently, touching the girl's shoulder.

Lila looked up into her blue eyes, startled. "Th-thank you. I think I'll be fine." She bit hard into the toast and felt all eyes on her still. She held the bread in front of her face, rudely.

Ron, though he still frightened her the most, had the most reasonable response. "I need a piss." He stood and walked from the room. Lila heard Grace sigh and murmur to him about manners on her way to the door.

Lila nearly fell off her chair when a hand touched her elbow on the table. Really, she was on her own only hours and she'd forgotten all her etiquette. Setting the toast down, she met George's brown eyes and licked crumbs from her lips.

He looked uncomfortable. "Do you ... Do you know what you plan to do now, Lila?"

She felt her throat tighten. He knew she wasn't going home, but she hadn't told him she couldn't. The truth was that she had no idea what to do next. She had a vague idea to go to another city, maybe as far as Nashville, and try to find work. That would mean living in the street, not the hardest thing at this time of year, she expected, but she didn't have the faintest idea how or where to start. She'd never had to take care of herself before.

"No," she answered honestly, breaking eye contact to look at and turn her toast with a finger. "I thought I'd go ... somewhere else. Start new."

His smile, soft before, broadened now. "I think that's a good idea. Are you particular where you go?" The smile slid a little, something else in his eyes now: worry? fear?

She shook her head. "No. My first thought was Nashville, but I'm not picky at all. I can't go to family," she muttered, picking up the toast to cover her hands shaking in anger. Her eyes met his. "You know, don't you?"

"About a possible baby?" he said, cocking his head to one side. "About being kicked out of your house? Yes, Lila. Grace gets word fast, and she heard that this was likely to happen, if ..." he broke off. Smile gone completely now, a growl entered his voice, "If James had defiled you. I swear, Lila, if I had known this would happen ..." He covered his eyes with one of his hands and his broad shoulders slumped.

He'd only been kind to her, this strange man. Showing her more care and love than anyone she had known before, she felt the overwhelming need to comfort him now. She stood, her chair scraping on the wood floor, and rounded the table to put her arms around his shoulders, hands barely meeting on the far one. He lifted one hand to touch her elbow, and she thought she heard him sob.

"George?" she asked. She had never seen a man cry before.

"He got you, Lila. I shouldn't have been the only one looking for him. If I'd told someone ..." he cried again, and this time Lila saw the tear fall.

"He didn't hurt me, George. He just left me," she tried to explain.

"Lila, you didn't want what he did to you, did you?" he asked, turning those sorrowful eyes to her. "You didn't chase him, did you?" His lip trembled a little.

Her throat caught, remembering that first day, a year ago. He had definitely been chasing. "No," she answered in a whisper.

George pushed his chair out from the table. He put an arm around her waist and hugged her back. "Neither did Daphne."

Daphne. That was the name of his daughter. Her lips compressed in a line. James had loved Lila; he had planned to marry her. She wasn't like this other girl. Pulling away from George slightly, he looked up.

"You could come home with me," George said quietly. "I talked to my wife this morning, and she agreed. If you need a place to stay, even just to get your feet under you, you can have it with us."

Lila's mouth fell open. That was a good offer.

George went on. "Colorado's cooler than here, but we can find you some clothes. You can stay until the baby, or longer. You'd have to share a room with Daphne or one of the other girls, maybe Janet."

"Are you serious?" she asked, astounded.

"Very," he said, squeezing her hand. "My family could have stopped this sooner. It is the least we can do now."

She pressed her lips together for a moment. "Can I have some time to think about it?" she asked.

"Of course!" George said, smiling again. "Take as much time as you need. Ron has said you can have the girls' room here."

"He has ... girls?" Someone had married that man? Her eyes went wide.

George nodded. "They live with their mother, but he keeps the room in hopes they'll visit one day. He's a trucker, though, so he's gone for months at a time. And I need to get back to work next week, so I'll only be here a few more days. I can leave you a bus ticket, though." He smiled again. It was disarming. She could feel herself smiling back.

"I don't think I'll need that long," she answered.

"I'm glad. We're on our own for lunch, but Grace serves supper at six." George smoothed a curl of her hair. "If you want to join us, that is," he added as an afterthought.

Lila felt her mouth curl up even further. "I'd love to join you," she said. Suddenly, her stomach turned sour. Her eyes went wide as she felt bile rising in her throat. With no idea where the bathroom was, she leaned over the kitchen sink, her toast coming back up.

The water was turned on while she still clutched the edge of the sink, knuckles white. Then, just as quickly, the nausea was gone. She saw a tumbler stuck under the stream and felt her hair was swept away.

The water level wobbled as she took the glass from a three-fingered hand. She looked up at Ron who smiled, the gaps in his teeth showing.

"Morning sick?" he said. "Don't worry, it passes."

"It usually passes." George was leaning on a counter on the other side. Ron must have gotten to her first. "Eva was sick for three months with Marlene. Thought she'd waste away on us."

Both these men were fathers. They both knew more about babies and being pregnant than she did. "What else? Is it only in the morning?"

Two heads shook. "If you're lucky, it only bothers you until noon. Eva was sick all day every day for those three months," George said, frowning.

"Karen didn't have it as bad as that, but for the month she was sick, it could come any time, morning, noon or night. Both girls," he added after, chuckling a little. It slipped. "I miss those babes," he murmured.

As his eyes softened, Lila saw something beyond the hard whiskered face, bald head, and missing teeth. Ron wasn't a hard man. She smiled at him before turning back to George. "How many children do you have?" she asked.

"Three, all girls. Daphne, she'll be turning eighteen soon. Marlene is pretty close to your age, I wager, and Janet is the baby. If you can call a thirteen year old that. Thirteen? When did I get three teenagers in my house?" he asked no one in particular.

Ron laughed at him. "And you just invited a fourth, all girls, saints preserve you."

Lila couldn't help but chuckle even though she was part of the joke. "So when will I ..." she held her hands out from her belly, "you know."

George chuckled. "If you just started getting sick, not for another couple months, that's about when you should start feeling it moving, too." He smiled warmly. Then his smile fell, and his brow creased. "You shouldn't have to learn that so soon."

She waved him off. "My mother was only seventeen when she had Christian. I'll be fine." It was true, but she wasn't nearly as confident as she tried to sound.

He smiled a little. "And Eva was only a year older than that. I suppose you're right. Just seems too young somehow." His frown deepened.

Lila, feeling awkward, rubbed one leg with the toes of the other. "Do you think I could use your shower?" she asked Ron, not quite meeting his eye. "Please?" she added.

He grinned. "Help yourself. Fresh towels are in the closet beside." He gestured to the stairs.

"Thank you," she said, slipping back to the pink room to grab a change of clothes. George and Ron were sitting on couch, exchanging baby stories by the sound of it.

She spent most of the day going through her few possessions and folding them properly. They'd still need ironing, but weren't in terrible shape. The final item, and the only one that wasn't clothing, now sat open in her lap.

A single knock preceded George poking his head in. "Nearly six, are you still..." When he saw the photo album, he cut off. "May I?" he asked, moving to sit beside her.

She shuffled a little to give him more room on the edge of the bed. "Christian thrust this at me as I ran out the door. I'm glad he did." There were tears on her cheeks. Things were simpler when she was little. She looked at pictures where she played next to her brother and remembered being happy.

Her mother looked cold and commanding even then, she noticed, and there were few photos of her father.

"Your brother?" he asked, pointing at Christian, swinging off a rope into the lake.

Lila smiled. "Yes. He ... well, he was the closest to me, I suppose." She closed the book and didn't look up at George. How could she explain that she felt as close to him after one day as she had to her brother?

"You'll miss him," George said, rubbing her back.

She nodded, but said nothing.

"Well, the house is just across the street, whenever you're ready."

Lila closed the album and stood. "I'm ready now," she said, pushing the memories, good and bad, aside. Smiling, she took George's hand.

He rubbed the back with his thumb and squeezed once. "No rush," he reminded her.

"I'm ready," she said, and her stomach growled, making her blush.

"So you are!" George held the door open for her and then led the way to the house across the street.

Lila froze just inside the door. She was used to quiet dinners with silverware and wine glasses. There were six people around the table, each holding a piece of chicken up to their lips and tearing the meat with their teeth. The boys, in particular, looked nearly feral as they attacked the birds.

"Lila!" Grace said, rising and wiping her hands on a cloth napkin. "Please, join us. Close your mouth when you chew," she told one of the boys, slapping the back of his head.

Lila swallowed and moved to take a seat. She sighed in relief upon finding fork and knife by her plate. She stabbed one of the pieces of chicken on the platter nearest her and put it on her plate. Ron passed her fried potatoes, which she heaped alongside. Coleslaw came next, finishing her meal. Using her knife, she cut off a piece of the meat and put it in her mouth.

She noticed the room become quiet as she chewed. What were they staring at?

"It's very good, Grace. Thank you for inviting me," she said, nodding her head to her hostess.

That seemed to stir everyone a little. "I'm glad you like it. I heard you were having trouble keeping things down. How is this so far?" She tore another strip of flesh from the bones in her hand.

Lila speared a potato and popped that in her mouth. She noticed everyone else using their fingers for these as well. The seasoning on them was spicy; she liked it. Swallowing, she paused, gauging her stomach. If it was like this morning, it would turn soon after the food made it there.

"No trouble at all," she said with a smile.

"Just mornings then. Good." Grace smiled at her before spearing a potato with her fork. "Don't mind these ruffians," she said, gesturing around the table. Even George was tearing into a piece of chicken with his teeth. "Their manners may not be as good as yours, but they're good boys."

The conversation may not have been quiet, but it was interesting. Lila didn't know anything about how to slingshot a magpie, or think it was necessarily a good topic for the table, but she did learn a lot. She also listened avidly as Izzy, the toddler, tried to tell her all about the story her friend's mother had told her, although, at some point, it became Izzy doing the things in the story. Lila encouraged the little girl, asking her what happened next, and making um and ah noises at the appropriate times.

By the time both chickens were completely devoured, Lila felt a bit less out of place with the group. Was George's family like this, she wondered, looking at him.

"Supper is a little less chaotic at our house," he told her quietly. "Certainly less bodies around the table." He winked.

She smiled, relieved to hear that. After dinner she walked back with Ron and George on either side of her.

"George?" she asked quietly as they reached the porch. "I think I'd like to go home with you."

He smiled broadly. "I'm glad. We'll head out in the morning."

Chapter Eleven

She was so young, so small, and having a baby. George admired Lila's courage. She slung her bag into the box of the truck and climbed in before waving to Ron and Grace, who stood on Ron's porch.

He would be seeing the trucker again, he was certain. If Ron ever found himself needing a stop-over in Colorado, he would be staying with the Kingston's. Grace ... George didn't know if he'd ever see her again. Like Mae, he hoped he would one day, but the odds weren't promising.

Lila sat back crossing her hands on her belly.

"Anything?" he asked, quirking an eyebrow and smiling.

"Not unless I'm having butterflies," she said with a smile of her own, her green eyes showing a little sparkle.

She didn't belong in his world. His family would be strange to her, though hopefully not as strange as Grace's brood. She had looked frightened at dinner last night. Still, she came from money, old money unless he missed his guess. She would be living a lot leaner in the days to come. On the bright side, it would be less lean than fending for herself.

The more he glanced at the girl from the corner of his eye, the more he thought she was thinking all the same things he was.

"He did love me," she murmured, stroking her belly.

Or maybe she wasn't. In either case, George had no answer to that.

The drive was very quiet. George tried a few times the first couple days to bring her out of her shell. He asked about school, what her favorite classes were. He asked more about her family, though he expected that one to fail. He asked about the places she'd seen, if she'd ever been to Colorado.

She answered politely, but never elaborated. For instance, she said she'd visited Colorado, Denver, but been two at the time and didn't remember it at all. She didn't offer any other places she'd been, or vacations she'd gone on. George didn't press her. It was a small cab and the drive was bad enough without making it awkward.

She asked him a few questions and he went on at length about each of his daughters, his wife, the school the girls were attending, where he expected Lila would likely go.

"I don't think I'll be going to school for a few months," she replied, holding her belly.

George nodded in understanding. "I suppose not. That will pass, though," he reminded her.

"And then I'll have a baby. Who will watch it while I go to class?" she asked.

He shut up for a while after that.

Still, the drive wasn't onerous, and the stops were frequent enough, letting them each stretch. It wasn't until the third day that a thought finally occurred to George.

"Would you like to drive a while, Lila?" he asked, holding out the keys.

She blinked. "I ... Yes, that would be nice. Thank you, George."

He smiled and hopped into the passenger side. Of course, this just made him restless so he peppered her with even more questions. Now they were much simpler though. What was her favorite song? Her favorite color? Her favorite season?

She caught on to him quick. "Are you building a file on me, George? I'm a Pisces, that might be important." Her smile warmed him. She still didn't smile enough.

As the third day dragged on, he thought over all he'd learned of her. He still felt he didn't know this girl at all. What did she really love?

"You're fast, you know that?" he told her, remembering trying to catch her at the Greene farm.

She grinned. "I love to run. My mother scolds me every time she sees me, so I make sure she doesn't see me," she said with a shrug. "James liked to chase me," her voice distanced a little. "He liked to catch me."

George wished he hadn't asked.

"Yours," she murmured, seeming to see through the road.

"Lila?" he asked.

She shook her head and smiled again. "He liked to run, too. Not as much as me, I think. I would never walk if I could. Nothing as good as stretching the legs, feeling my hair stream out, listening to the thud of feet." Her eyes were dreamy now, then saddened. "Though except for chasing a little one ..." She rubbed her belly again.

George brushed her arm. "I'm sure you'll find plenty of other reasons to run. Hell, you don't need a reason at all."

She grinned at that. "Open space is reason enough," she said.

He nodded. He had helped. This was a start. He needed to do more, but this was a start.

***

Patty lifted her head slowly, the light painful to her eyes. The room was disgusting, a pot in the corner for a toilet and only a cot to sleep on. She rolled off and was surprised at the bars.

"Patricia Wood?" a male voice said, ringing in her ears.

"Yes?" she croaked, her throat parched.

"You're free to go now." The bars she hadn't looked at yet swung out. "Try to stay clothed in public in future." The man in the uniform eyed her sadly.

"Yeah, I'll do that," she answered snidely. "Where are my things?"

He snorted. "You weren't even wearing that when you came in." He gestured to the leather jacket she wore. It just covered her hips although there was nothing beneath it. We pulled that out of the Lost and Found."

"Then how do you know my name?" she asked, squinting at him.

He shook his head. "You've been here enough times, Patty. We know you. Go home, clean up. I'm sure your Mom and Dad will be happy to see you."

That meant she was home, in Fort Garland. She'd left, once she was sure James wouldn't come looking for her. Why had she come back? She hadn't been in this particular cell in over a year. The last time had been because she'd passed out in the park. James had beaten her hard for that. Didn't want her wasting time in a cell when he had need of her. She pulled the coat tighter around her and tossed her head as she marched out of the precinct.

She was not going back to her parents' house. They'd had no time for her when she lived there, too busy with six other mouths to feed. Hitting the street, she went straight to Mick's. He was old and ornery, but he was also quick to give a twenty for a good blow. With that, she'd get some pants, then she'd get out of town. It didn't hurt that he always had some weed either.

She watched Nancy Spencer gape at her. Sneering, Patty pulled the jacket up and rubbed herself once before flipping the bitch the bird.

She'd spent lots of time at the Spencer house, until Nancy had decided she wasn't good enough for James. She had been the first to call her worthless, make her feel worthless. Well, Nancy wasn't worth anything either, certainly not her time. Unless James was back.

Patty had already gone three blocks, but she turned, searching every alley, every window. When she was sure she didn't see him anywhere, she ran the rest of the way to Mick's. The sooner she was out of here, the better.

The old man opened the door while she was still banging her fist on it, a cigarette dangling from his lips. "Patty Wood? Would if she could?"

"You have the wood," she replied, lifting her jacket up. "You got the bread, too?" she asked, stepping past him.

"For you, delicious, I can find some."

Chapter Twelve

Lila pulled her bag slowly from the back of the truck and walked up the steps behind George, anxious about what was to come. He had tried to help her feel better on the drive, but she was still the stranger here; he was coming home. She looked at the small white house. Could it be her home?

She didn't dare hope for that. It would be enough if it were a place to start. George pushed open the door and was tackled by a girl with bouncing ashen curls. Hugging his daughter in return, George laughed.

"Janet, love, I missed you too," he said, trying to take a step with the girl fastened to him.

"Then let me finish welcoming you," Janet complained.

This was the youngest, Lila had learned, the most exuberant, the most outgoing, the loudest. Apparently she was also the most affectionate and least likely to bend as well. George slowly pried her fingers from around him so he could kiss the light haired woman who wore an apron.

"Just in time for dinner," his wife, Eva told him. "And you would be Lila," she said, taking Lila's shoulders into her hands and squeezing them gently. Lila tried not to shift or flinch at the unexpected contact. "I'm happy you came. I hope you like it here."

"I'm sure I will," Lila answered, not knowing if that was even likely.

The two girls standing at the counter both had wavy brown hair, the shorter of the two turned and dropped a parer into the sink. "Thank goodness you're home. Still a couple weekends," she said, seemingly reminding George of something.

"Yes, Muffet. I'll try to take you out to the lake. I have work, too," he told her.

Muffet? Lila hadn't heard him refer to any of the girls by that name in their conversations. Was this Marlene or Daphne?

A young man, a little older than herself, came into the kitchen. He walked over to the girl still at the counter and kissed her head. That would be Adam, making the girl Daphne. Those two seemed intent on each other, but all the other eyes were on her.

"Stop staring," George chided his younger daughters. "Talk to her."

"Hello," Janet said first. "Dad said you're going to be living here?" She seemed confused by that.

"Just for a while," Lila answered. "Until I find my feet."

Janet's brow creased, but she didn't say any more.

Marlene introduced herself. "Are you ... sort of like a sister?" she asked. "I mean," she started, looking at her parents, "you're going to be part of the family, right? Like a sister?" Lila couldn't quite fathom that.

"Maybe more like a cousin," George offered. That was easier. She had plenty of cousins she'd only met once or twice.

"I'm Daphne," she said, coming forward and standing between Lila and her sisters. "You'll be staying in my room. Why don't you bring your things and follow me? *Some* people need to get supper ready," she said, looking pointedly at her siblings. Marlene grimaced and Janet stuck out her tongue.

"Adam," George said to the young man, shaking his hand. "Anything happen while I was gone?" The way he talked to him, the way he talked of him, made it clear he already thought of him as a son. Did he see Lila as a daughter? No, she thought, probably just a niece. She fell back to the cousin analogy.

Daphne opened one of the doors on the second floor. The room had two dressers and a double bed. There was just enough room to walk past the dressers without turning sideways and a little space at the foot of the bed near the closet.

"I don't do anything in here but sleep," Daphne said, sitting on the foot of the bed. "I had to push this against the wall to make room for your dresser. We'll have to share bed and closet."

Lila had never shared a bed with anyone, not that she could recall. She hadn't slept with James either, always spirited back to her room, alone. She'd shared motel rooms with George, but always separate beds. Even that had been difficult; she noticed his breathing every time she tossed. What would it be like sharing a bed with Daphne, she wondered.

"I can go," the older girl said, rising. "Let you unpack."

"No," Lila whispered. "You can stay." She had best get used to the older girl. Opening her sack, Lila pulled out the pile that needed ironing the most and set it in front of the closet, then she put the less wrinkled items in the drawer: denim jeans (she only had one pair of those) and corduroy skirts. Finally she set her underclothes, stockings and socks in the top of her drawers, tucking the album in among them. Hopefully no one would go snooping there.

"You don't have much. If you need anything, we're close enough to the same size. Skirts rather than pants, you're taller," Daphne observed.

Lila looked at the girl out of the corner of her eye, really judging her for the first time. She was dressed simply, but well. She had beautiful brown hair that curled around her face, obscuring it a little from view, but one of her large brown eyes was visible, watching almost as closely. They were like two cats, each testing the territory for dominance.

Licking her lips, Lila closed the drawer. She was pretty sure Daphne was a timid person, someone her mother would walk all over and instruct Lila to do the same.

"Do you mind if I take the outside of the bed?" Lila asked.

"Not at all," Daphne said, rising and smoothing her skirt. Lila was right. The inside of the bed would both be colder and inconvenient if one had to rise in the night, yet she gave it up quickly and easily. No wonder James had found her easy to mold.

What was she thinking?! That was an awful thought. James didn't use people, women, like that. He loved her.

She felt heat in her cheeks from her embarrassment and anger at herself. She was spared when Eva called for dinner. Following Daphne down the stairs, Lila was nearly bowled over by Janet coming from behind.

"Sorry," she called over her shoulder, not slowing. What would Lila's mother have said if she'd run like that through the house?

Lila shook her head. She wasn't in her mother's house anymore and she needed to start accepting that. Smiling, she thought maybe the lax rules would be nice. Standing to one side, she watched George and Eva sit at one end of the table, Adam and Daphne at the other. Daphne was next to her mother, leaving three chairs on the other side. Janet took the middle and Marlene paused, watching her.

"Why don't you sit beside Dad?" Marlene suggested.

Lila smiled gratitude at her. She would be more comfortable next to George, who she knew, than Adam, who she'd just met. She bowed her head with the rest of the family for George's simple blessing.

"...and bless Lila. Help her to find her place with us soon. Amen."

Her head came up. Why had he prayed that? Wasn't this just a stop-over for her? Somewhere to gather herself before facing the world? He made it sound like she was part of the family.

Moved, she was slow to take the bowl of salad from Janet, but eventually got into the rhythm of dishes circling the table.

After dinner she started to help clean up. Daphne stopped her.

"You don't need to help tonight, Lila. I saw you had a pile of ironing. Mom can show you where the iron is."

Eva rose and put an arm around Lila's shoulders. "I can. I can iron some, too, if the pile is too big." She opened a closet and pulled down an electric steam iron, plugging it in and folding down the ironing board from its cupboard in the kitchen. It made the kitchen crowded, Lila ironing while Daphne washed and Adam dried, but it wasn't too bad.

Adam had a scar in his eyebrow. She spotted it as she swapped one blouse for another, placing the pressed one on a hanger. Another glance showed her that his nose was broken as well. Only once, and he didn't have any other scars. He was tall and thin; she didn't think he was a fighter.

He caught her looking. "They're from James," he said, tapping his eyebrow and then pointing out another scar below his ear.

Lila had no response to that. Returning to her chore, she tried not to look at him any longer. She expected they would leave as soon as the dishes were finished, but instead, they stayed in the kitchen, talking in whispers. Adam kissed Daphne, and it reminded Lila of James. Except his kisses were almost never little pecks like that.

Daphne pulled away at one point, taking Adam to the door. It was later than Lila supposed. She wouldn't finish her ironing tonight and gathered up the hangers she'd filled, carrying them to her new bedroom.

Eva stood in the doorway when Lila turned to retrieve the rest of her clothes. The now smaller pile was in the older woman's arms.

"Can I talk to you, Lila?" she asked, handing over the bundle.

"Um, yes, of course."

Eva moved to sit on the bed and waited for Lila to join her. The older woman had lines at the corners of her eyes and mouth. She wasn't smiling now, but it was obvious she did often.

"Lila, I let my daughter down. There were signs I should have seen pointing to what Daphne kept hidden, but I didn't see them. I can't fix what happened to Daphne, but I was hoping you would let me help you."

"Help me?" Lila asked.

"George told me how suddenly your mother kicked you out of the house. I imagine you feel a little lost now, without either of your parents. It's probably way too soon to mention this, but George and I would be happy to think of you as a fourth daughter. We both care about you Lila, and want to make sure you feel that you aren't restricted by what happened to you. Does that make any sense?" Eva paused, watching Lila's reaction.

She was shocked. They really wanted her to be part of their family? They cared what happened to her? Who were they? Why should they care?

Daphne. They still thought their situations were similar. Eva confirmed that with her next words.

"Daphne has been talking to a counsellor, someone to help her work through what happened to her. If you'd like, we can set you up to see her as well. George's union pays for it, so it wouldn't be a problem at all."

"They wouldn't pay for me, though," Lila argued. She wasn't actually their daughter.

"No, but we can afford yours because we don't pay for Daphne's."

Lila continued to shake her head. They would pay for her to talk to someone? They would pay for her to see a doctor for the baby, she realized in the same moment. She had no way of doing that. Looking at Eva, Lila had new respect for her.

"Thank you," she said, choking up. "I still don't understand why you'd do all this for me, but thank you."

Eva hugged her then. Lila froze for a moment. When was the last time she'd had a hug? James. But from family? Her father hugged her ... sometimes. Christian, she remembered. He would hug her like this. He just hadn't since ... she turned thirteen or so. Somehow it became improper then. Why? Why wouldn't her mother and brother hug her?

She hugged Eva back, arms tight around her waist and head against the older woman's collarbone. Then she felt the tears prickling. She started to pull away, but Eva held her close, patting and smoothing her hair.

"Cry, sweetie. You've lost a lot. It has to be hard."

Lila wasn't crying for what she'd lost. It was true, she had lost her family, her name, but she'd gained a family that showed love and affection for one another, people who would hold her up when the world tried to pull her down.

However, she couldn't explain that to Eva. She just kept thinking about George's warm brown eyes and that moment in Ron's kitchen when she'd felt not just wanted but cared for.

Another person came in and sat on Lila's other side, stroking her back. It was Daphne, Lila saw as she turned her head.

With another pat, Daphne rose and began unbuttoning her blouse. Eva rose, taking Lila's hands.

"It's late," Eva said, "Sleep well, Lila. We can talk more tomorrow." Then she kissed Lila's forehead and Daphne's cheek. "Goodnight, girls."

She said it as though they really were sisters. Lila was startled when Janet came in and bounced on the bed to hug her as well. "Goodnight, Lila. See you in the morning. 'Night, Daph," she said, hugging her sister before racing out of the room.

Lila had only just collected herself when Marlene came in and hugged them both as well. This was going to take some time to get used to. She rose and started pulling off her sundress. Daphne had pulled on a short night dress and was pulling back the covers when a quick knock sounded on the door.

"One minute," Daphne said, gesturing to Lila to finish.

She did, dropping the dress and removing her brassiere quickly before tugging the night gown over her head.

"Come in," Daphne said.

"Just wanted to wish you both good night." George looked a little awkward in the doorway. He was flushed as though he realized what he'd almost walked in on. Eventually he shuffled in to hug and kiss Daphne, then did the same to Lila.

She couldn't handle the emotion rising in her. As she had with Eva, she clutched this rough and tumble man who had found her, picked her up, and brought her into his home, his family. His peck on the cheek had been the confirmation of what she'd seen in his eyes days ago. He loved and cared for her. Not the way James had, the way a father would.

"Lila? Are you okay?" he asked, still holding her, stroking her back. She felt his head turn, probably to look at Daphne, whiskers rubbing her cheek.

"Yes. I'm better than okay. I'm going to be perfect." She sniffed the tears back, wiping her face with the back of her hand.

"You are perfect now," George said. He couldn't know that. Still, she appreciated the sentiment. Raising onto tip toe, she kissed his bristly cheek in return.

She watched the door for a minute, holding onto the moment, until the rustle of blankets drew her attention. She flipped off the light and climbed in beside Daphne.

"We're both going to be okay," Daphne murmured, rubbing Lila's arm before turning to face the wall. "He can't hurt us anymore."

Lila didn't respond to that. She lay, looking at the ceiling and then moved her hand down, slipping it into the panties she still wore.

A hand closed on her wrist and she jumped a little.

"Whose?" Daphne said.

Lila's mouth fell open. She had known James. "Yours," she answered without thinking.

"No," Daphne insisted, squeezing Lila's wrist. "Yours." Releasing the hand, she rolled to the wall again.

"Mine?" Lila whispered. Daphne turned over again, a sad smile on her face.

"It will take a while to get used to that, I know. And it'll be a week at least before you stop touching yourself every night. He's not here, Lila. He won't know if you don't. You get to choose when you want to do it, now. It's yours. Took me months to figure that out, but hopefully you can get there faster." She slipped her elbow under her head and closed her eyes again. Lila could only tell because the faint street light had been reflected in them. She turned away from Daphne and tried to close her own eyes, unable to shake the feeling of being watched and at the same time knowing she wasn't. Sleep was elusive.

Chapter Thirteen

Lila was fitting right in. George was thrilled. The day after he got home, he took Daphne and Adam to the police station to file a report on James. Both said they were ready to report the incident, ready to stop James legally.

"We've been talking about it for a while now," Adam said, looking at Daphne as he spoke.

"I'm ready, Daddy," Daphne told him confidently. "I can't ... tell everyone, but I'm ready to tell more people."

The filing was late, and the Sergeant warned that it might not come to much, but it was done. Next he took them to a lawyer. Well, a law student. They weren't swimming in money, but Luke Anderson was taking his bar exam in the next few months, so he was eager to have clients. His rates were more than reasonable. He had redirected them to the district attorney's office.

George left the young couple with the DA and drove to the site where Joe had the crew working this week.

"You finally back, you old fart?" Joe asked.

"Old?" George asked, raising a brow. "Mick's old." The man named snorted where he worked a circular saw.

Joe laughed in agreement. "You back then? Find what you needed in Knoxville?"

"I did. Brought back a nice girl, down on her luck. So ... I have another mouth to feed. I'd better get back to work!" He smiled.

Joe slapped his back. "I'll say. See you at seven?" he asked.

George nodded. "Happily. Looking good," he mused, eying the foundation that had been laid and the struts already up.

Joe shrugged. "Not the most difficult job we've had. You weren't looking to work now, were you?" he asked, looking oddly at George's slacks and dress shirt.

George chuckled. "No. Just had an appointment with a lawyer is all. Thought it would be better if I didn't wear the work gear."

Joe nodded, but lowered his voice. "A lawyer? Anything wrong?"

George nodded. "Daphne and her new beau, Adam, ran into trouble with Josh Spencer's younger son, James. We're finally filing charges against him." He kept his voice low, too, though the news would spread quickly. Exactly the reason they hadn't done this sooner.

"Spencer, eh? Can't say I'm surprised his kids turned out to be rotten apples. Hope things work out."

"Me too," George agreed, nodding. "But I'll be here in the morning. Need to go pick the kids up."

"Sure, we'll see you then. Take care, George."

"See ya, George!" he heard a few workers cry to him. He waved to them as he got back in his truck.

***

Blood flowed down the side of her head into her hair. She wasn't sure what she'd done to piss him off. She wasn't sure why he'd left her here, but she was sure she was still alive. Dead wouldn't hurt as much.

Pushing herself to her knees, Patty looked around. She was outside, as usual, in an alley. At least she had some clothes, even if they were caked with mud and who knew what else. Probably vomit. She could taste that along with the blood.

She made it to her feet slowly and staggered down the alley to the street, one hand braced on the brick wall. She was behind the bar. Leaning on the wall for a moment, she peered the other way, to the clock on the post office. It was noon. She pulled herself around the corner and opened the door.

"Patty," Waylon said, throwing his cloth down on the bar. "I swear, I should never let you in here again."

"Yeah, yeah, just let me use the can."

He didn't say anything else, just went back to cleaning.

The mirror was cracked, but showed her truly. Sallow skin, bruises covering half her face, a nose crooked and swollen. Her stringy yellow hair was half-caked with blood, matted to her cheek. Reaching into a pocket of her leather jacket, she was relieved to find her knife. So many johns felt the need to empty her pockets. The knife really freaked them out. She slipped the jacket to the grimy floor.

Pulling locks away from her face, she sawed through one after another, after another. It was a rough job and she had odd lengths, but they were all short and stuck out. It made her look ... mean. She could use that. Running water in the sink, she washed her hair and face until the water ran clear. Then she stripped off her shirt and wadded up some paper towel to clean her torso. When she felt closer to human, she checked the gash on her temple. A thin stream of blood ran from it, but there was nothing she could do. She couldn't afford a doctor. She tore off a scrap of the paper towel and held it until the blood congealed. It would have to do.

She stepped out of the washroom, shrugging her jacket back on.

"Wow," Waylon murmured. "That's some hair. Between that, the face and the scars on your knuckles, no one's going to pick a fight with you, even if you do still look skinny enough to blow away on the next breeze."

She chuckled. "Good. I don't want any more fights." Her stomach turned, hunger probably, but she'd learned to ignore that long ago. "What I do want is a way out of here. I was supposed to be out of this piss-pot town weeks ago. You know anyone I can hitch a ride with? You know how I can pay." She smirked at him. Waylon didn't go for girls, which was fine by her.

He shook his head. "I got nothing, sorry kid. Though, y'know, I've offered you a job here before. Would you take it now?"

"Even though I have nowhere to stay?" she asked, quirking a brow.

He shrugged. "You don't seem interested in booze; you can sleep behind the bar for all I care."

He was right. Alcohol did nothing for her. She could get drunk faster than anyone, but it didn't give her the lift the drugs did. It was those she needed. She'd never be able to pay for them with what she would make here. Waylon knew that.

"For now," she said, tentative.

"For now," he agreed.

Chapter Fourteen

Lila walked timidly into Mrs. Peterson's office. She'd expected it to be something like a doctor's office, sterile, but it was nothing of the sort. There was no desk, no table, or not a large table, just a short coffee table. Two china teacups sat next to a sugar bowl and cream pitcher; steam rose from one. Three of the four walls were bookcases. Most of the shelves held novels, a few textbooks, and many photos and figurines.

"Lila Everett?" the gray-haired woman asked. She lifted her glasses up her nose slightly to peer with blue eyes. She rose gracefully despite her considerable girth and took Lila's hand. "I'm Wanda. It's a pleasure to meet you."

She didn't want to be called Mrs. Peterson? Lila was surprised. With an effort she said. "It's a pleasure to meet you ... Wanda."

"Do you drink tea?" Mrs. Peterson asked, gesturing to the teapot on the table. "Orange Pekoe."

"Yes, please," Lila answered, following the older woman's lead in taking a seat on one of the two couches. The one Mrs. Peterson sat on was more of a love seat than a sofa, whereas Lila sat against a cushion on a bench made for three.

After the tea was poured and prepared, both women sat back and sipped. Mrs. Peterson sighed audibly. "Tell me, Lila, what is your favorite tea?"

Lila's brow crinkled. This was supposed to be a therapy session, right? "Uh, I like Earl Grey, actually, but this is probably my second favorite."

Mrs. Peterson nodded. "Earl Grey is very good. I prefer it in the morning though. Orange Pekoe ... reminds me afternoons in summer, not unlike this one, but outside, under a willow tree." Her blue eyes seemed to grow distant and then focused on Lila again. "What does tea remind you of?"

Lila's mind immediately went back to her parents' yard. Afternoon tea with all the ladies around a long table, chatting and snacking, sipping and gossiping. The china in her hand, the smell of the tea, it was all the same.

The cup hit the floor, spilling on the carpet.

"Oh my," Lila gasped. "I'm so sorry." She jumped up looking for a way to clean it up.

Mrs. Peterson pulled a rag from behind one of the framed photos. In the photo her arm was around a younger man with dark hair. She squatted and sopped up the tea. "It's no trouble, my dear, but you've made me extra curious." Her eyes sparkled when they met Lila's.

"My mother would host afternoon tea every Sunday," Lila began. "I never liked them. She made sure my brother and I were dressed in the prettiest, least comfortable clothes, and then we would stand around for hours while they just talked." Lila rested her chin in one hand.

Mrs. Peterson nodded. "I see. Definitely more of an adult gathering than a child's. Though I'm guessing you threw many a tea party of your own. For your dolls?"

Lila shook her head. "I was too busy outside, climbing trees, running." She sighed quietly. "I love to run."

Mrs. Peterson smiled at her, sipping her tea. "Do you? Where did you run? And help yourself to more tea if you'd like," she offered.

Lila poured herself another cup, fixing it how she liked, cream with just a touch of sugar. She leaned into the cushion at her back. "Everywhere, anywhere. My yard most often. Down the hill to the creek. Across the farmers fields to the west. Up to the church." She paused, sipping. Then giggled. "The vicar was scandalized when he found me racing up and down the graveyard."

"Racing a ghost?" Mrs. Peterson asked, smile broad, showing pearly teeth. Lila was sure they were false.

She nodded. "Pretending to, anyway." She sipped again. "Mother put a stop to that. She said ladies didn't run and made my life miserable every time she caught me."

Mrs. Peterson nodded. "My mother was much the same. Propriety first."

"But who cares?" Lila asked. "Why should it matter if a girl wears a skirt or slacks? Why should it matter if she runs in public? Who made those rules anyway?" Her eyes widened as she realized what she was saying, who she was saying it to.

"An excellent question. I'll make you a deal. You find out, and I'll tar and feather him." Her grin was infectious and Lila smiled back. "Although, I prefer skirts to slacks, something simpler about them. No unfastening or care getting each leg in right, just pull it up." She let out one loud laugh and watched Lila for a reaction.

Still smiling, she didn't have one. Each were good for different reasons. She liked slacks for climbing and running; skirts tended to tangle. On the other hand, she wouldn't wear anything else to school.

School, it was starting next week. She wasn't attending, but that just meant she'd be home alone with Eva all day, every day ...

"The leaves are starting to turn," Mrs. Peterson mused, looking out the window. "Do you enjoy the autumn?"

Lila nodded, sipping again. "Not as much as summer, but I love the colors."

"Are you attending this year?" Mrs. Peterson asked, sipping from her cup.

She knew, of course. Daphne probably told her. "No," Lila answered. "I'm expecting a baby this winter."

As Lila had expected, Mrs. Peterson merely blinked. "Is that so? Young to be a mother, aren't you, only fifteen?"

Lila's mouth dropped. Up until now she'd told everyone she was sixteen, but in truth, she wouldn't be until her next birthday. "How did you ..." She shook her head. "Yes, it is young, but not too young. I'll be sixteen when the baby comes, and my mother was only a little older when she had my brother." Lila straightened her back, accepting the challenge.

"Yes, but she had a husband. Do you?"

It felt like a slap. "No. I was supposed to, but I guess George scared him off." Mrs. Peterson merely regarded Lila, waiting for her to continue. Slowly she did. "James is the father of my baby," she began. "He ... he taught me about being a woman."

"Did he now?" Mrs. Peterson said very quietly. "Go on, dear," she added, a little louder.

"He loved me and told me he would keep me forever. He was almost ready to talk to my father, but he wanted me to be a little older, so our age difference wouldn't seem so vast," she explained.

"Oh? It was more than is common?" Mrs. Peterson asked.

"Yes. He was over twenty. I never minded though," Lila said with a little chuckle. "Like I said, he taught me."

"So you did," the gray-haired woman murmured. Lila found her attention drawn to the red belt she wore on her blue printed dress. "And you sought these ... lessons?" she asked.

Lila clicked her tongue. George had made her face this earlier. "No, but I didn't abhor them. I wasn't hurt at all, except ..." Lila trailed off, not wanting to accept that there had been exceptions, that she had been hurt.

Her knees had been badly torn from falling when he chased her that first time. Those were her fault though, for running so hard. There had been pain a few times when she touched herself, but again, she inflicted that on herself.

There was the scar on her back.

Lila refused to face any of it, shaking her head. Mrs. Peterson hadn't moved, watching her. "I'm sure he was a good teacher, guiding you slowly."

Smiling at this, Lila answered, "Yes. He gave me time to learn one lesson before teaching another."

Mrs. Peterson's smile didn't fade. "You know that Daphne visits me as well. James taught her, too."

Lila nodded; she knew that. She'd learned more of it over the nights they'd shared a bed. She had many of the same rituals but wasn't following them as closely anymore.

"He is a very good teacher, but it is possible to unlearn, Lila. If you wish, I can show you how. Help you reverse the lessons he taught you." Her eyes were strong now, determined.

Lila licked her lips. "I don't know that I need to unlearn anything."

Mrs. Peterson's smile returned. "Of course, dear. Did you know James told Daphne he'd keep her forever as well? Told her that he would make sure that any man who knew her would know she was his?"

Lila's mouth went dry. It couldn't be true, could it? James loved her. He hadn't loved Daphne; that was why he left.

Several minutes passed as Lila tried to comprehend what the woman had just told her. The room was silent but for the occasional sip of tea and the ticking of the clock.

"Lila?" Mrs. Peterson finally asked. "You didn't know," she said. "It's true. He made sure no one else touched Daphne, making her his alone. Was it the same for you?"

Lila still didn't answer. Her tea sat on the table, cold now. Her mouth didn't seem to be working.

"Lila?" Mrs. Peterson asked again gently. Lila shook herself, regarding the older woman who smiled at her. "Can you tell me?"

"Yes. It was the same. Isn't it time to go?" she asked, looking for the clock she could hear. Eventually she found it on one of the shelves, but it was small and far away. She couldn't read it.

"Not quite. There was one more thing I wanted to mention, before time gets away on us. You don't have to go through with this pregnancy. It used to be, you wouldn't have a choice, but you do now. It is possible to end it."

She simply looked at her, not comprehending. End it? Take the baby? But it wasn't a baby yet. So ... it would die? She wrapped her arms around herself, not sure how to respond.

Lila remembered her mother complaining about something like this, dead babies and men playing God. She'd only been twelve and hadn't paid attention. Could she really stop being pregnant? The more she thought about it, the more impossible it seemed. However, she'd already accepted the permanency of this; she would have the baby, though she knew she couldn't keep it.

Adoption was something she did know about. Lila remembered the scandal when her neighbor had adopted a baby girl, and how everyone had tried to keep it from Lizzy. Her baby could be adopted. That would be for the best.

"I don't think I want that," she answered truthfully, several minutes later.

"Well, you have a few more weeks if you change your mind, but I'm happy to hear you know what you want. Our time is up, I'm afraid. Thank you for coming, Lila. I'll see you again on Friday." She pulled out a pad of paper and began writing furiously.

"Thank you, Mrs. Peterson," Lila answered, walking to the door.

"Wanda, Lila. Call me Wanda."

***

Lila decided to try talking to Daphne more. It had been made clear that she had a better idea of what Lila was feeling than she had first believed.

"Daphne? How did you meet James?"

She closed her eyes, seemingly reluctant to answer. Lila sat on the porch near Daphne and Adam in the swing. He took Daphne's hand now, patting it.

Her smile was thin, but Adam seemed appeased by it. She answered Lila, "He found me in the park, the one behind the church, where the lilacs grow around the edge. He said he'd never seen such a beautiful spring day, or shared one with such a beautiful girl. Then he gripped my hand and told me that he would hate for such a perfect day to slip away from him." Daphne stopped talking and looked down. After a moment she said, "He told me that he would make sure he held onto that day forever."

Lila nodded. Very different from her dangerous game of tag.

Adam stroked Daphne's arm, and she stiffened a little before relaxing into the caress. Lila was intruding on their time together. She rose, smiling to them both. "Thank you. I'll probably ask you more later."

Daphne reached out for her hand as she passed and squeezed it. Lila smiled at the gesture.

Lila decided to take care of herself while the room was unoccupied. Closing the door, she pulled off the panties from under her dress. Then she sat back on the bed and closed her eyes. She imagined James watching through the window, pretended he was still that close, pretending he had never gone.

Her body responded slowly, as it always did. She never understood why it was so hard for her enjoy this. There had certainly been times that she had, the times he put his mouth on her. Remembering helped; she needed to remember that. Her body seemed to relax and return the same sensations it had felt then, the tingle up her spine, the butterflies in her stomach.

Her lips parted in a gasp when she circled the bud, her fingers now wet. They seemed to burn as they rubbed, and she buried them in her again, feeling her need to squeeze.

The door opened suddenly, startling her.

"Daphne, I ..." Marlene stood in the doorway. She froze in place, turned bright red, and closed the door.

Lila groaned and straightened her skirt. She might as well wash her hands; the moment was gone. Opening the door, she nearly stepped on Marlene. She was still crimson faced.

"I'm really sorry, Lila. I ..." she paused and looked at her feet. Lila had to remind herself that she was only a little older than this girl. "Do you ..." Marlene finally walked away, never asking her question. Lila shook her head and continued to the bathroom.

Marlene was sitting on the bed when Lila returned to the room she shared with Daphne. Marlene held one of Daphne's stuffed bears. "You're my sister, right, Lila?" Marlene asked.

Lila sat and crossed her legs. She took one of Marlene's hands from the bear and squeezed it. "I suppose I am," she said with a small smile. She had never had a sister before, as much as she had wanted one. Now she had three, if she was willing to accept them. It was easier and easier to do that every day.

Marlene smiled back. "I ... Can I do that? I mean, Janet's in the room and so I usually do it in the tub, but is it okay?" She looked concerned.

Lila smiled at her. "It's fine."

"I won't ... lose my virginity or something?" she asked, still clutching the bear in her arms.

Lila's smile faded. "No. I was still a virgin when ..." She remembered the pain, the tearing, the blood. She swallowed carefully. James had been right, the next time hadn't hurt as much.

Marlene let out a heavy breath. "Good. I didn't want to ask Mom, and Daphne's ... Well, she has a hard enough time with Adam. I didn't think I could ask her."

Lila nodded, remembering Daphne's stiffness. "I thought it was just because I was there."

Marlene shook her head. "I watched from the window when he tried to kiss her one night. She ... got upset and ran back into the house."

"Oh." Lila didn't know what to say. "Well, she would have told you the same."

Marlene nodded. "I was pretty sure she knew, but, well, I didn't want to bring up any bad things. Why is it a bad thing, Lila? I mean, it's part of us, right?"

Lila didn't feel like she should be the one answering these questions. "I don't know."

Marlene sighed and hugged the bear again. "Well, if it's not going to hurt anything, I'm going to keep doing it. It feels good." Standing, she set the bear back on the shelf where it belonged and left.

Lila stayed in place, thinking. Was it wrong? Why would Daphne have trouble kissing Adam? Because she thought of James? That would make sense. Was that the problem with touching herself, too? She'd told Lila he wasn't watching anymore, that he wouldn't know if she didn't.

She put on a nightgown and went downstairs to wish Eva and George a good night.

The days with Eva were simpler than Lila had expected. She felt she should find some sort of work, but Eva pushed mention of that away.

"Help me get the chores out of the way, and I'll have more time for the work I do," she said with a grin. "Maybe you can help me." She pulled out a quilt that was missing six squares. Underneath were the pencil drawn designs she planned to stitch on. "These have been selling well. I'd love to be able to get more than one done in a month."

"I can definitely help with this," she said, fingering the delicate stitching. "Well, the quilting anyway. I don't know that I can embroider this well."

Eva also walked with her to the doctor two weeks after she moved in. "Our family doctor is Gray. He said he'd be happy to take you as well. Don't tell anyone, but he's going to list your appointments as mine. Everything but the actual birth should be paid by George's union coverage." Eva smiled broadly.

Lila felt her stomach ease. She hadn't known how she would afford a doctor and didn't expect it of her new family. If they didn't have to pay for all of it, she could accept their gift.

Eva also took Lila to thrift stores. Lila argued that she'd brought enough clothes to last a while.

"Yes, but they'll stop fitting soon. You need clothes that you'll only wear for a few months. Used is perfect," she explained, lifting a skirt with an elastic waistband.

Understanding, Lila started prowling the racks, looking at skirts and slacks two or three sizes too large. Eva brought over a few blouses that were a size large.

"Why-"

"You'll get bigger there too," Eva said hugging her shoulders. "And you won't want anything tight."

Milk. Milk in her breasts. "What if I don't keep the baby?" she asked, not meeting Eva's face. "What happens to the milk?"

She shrugged. "If no one drinks it, it stops coming. I weaned the girls off after a year, and by then, they weren't nursing much anymore. I imagine it would be harder if you never nursed." She looked at Lila. "You aren't planning on keeping the baby?"

Lila pulled a loose fitting dress off the rack, holding it up to herself. The green and blue went well with her coloring. "I can't take care of myself and a baby," she said simply.

Eva hugged her shoulders, kissing Lila's temple. "Silly girl, we'll take care of both of you. You're part of the family now."

Lila felt tears prick her eyes. This family, taking such good care of her, much better than her blood had treated her. She turned and clutched Eva, hugging her fiercely.

"Thank you," she whispered. "I ... I don't know ... what I ... would have done ..."

"Shh," Eva soothed, stroking Lila's hair and tucking her head under her chin. "It's alright, sweetie. You never have to know, now."

Chapter Fifteen

George used directory assistance to call Mae in Kingman.

"Hello?" a female voice answered.

"Hello, Mae! It's George Kingston, do you remember me?"

"This is Cindy," the girl said slowly. "Who is this?"

"Who is it?!" he heard Phillip yell.

"Shhh!" Cindy hushed him loudly.

"George. You had a note from your Mom for me? Phillip might remember."

"I don't know ..." Cindy sounded sceptical.

"Who is it!" Phillip yelled again.

"George!" she said in a huff.

"Hi George!" Phillip yelled. "Oh!" he said, sounding startled. "Cool, she gave me the phone."

"Heh, how are you, Phillip?"

"Oh! You're that George. I'm good. Did you find that guy?"

"No, actually, that was why I was calling."

"Oh," Phillip said. "Well, Mom won't be home until nine. Do you want her to call you back?" he asked.

"That's all right. I'll call her. Anything else new?"

"I made the baseball team," Phillip said proudly.

"That's great. Lots of practices?" It was nice to know the boy was doing well.

"Yep, three days a week. Mom says it keeps me out of her hair," he replied dryly.

George chuckled. "I'll bet she does. How is she?"

"Good. She quit her job at the grocer. She has enough work at the diner now. She's home more nights now, too." Phillip sounded thrilled with that. "You just picked a bad night. She'd be home tomorrow at this time."

"Well, I don't seem to have any luck, do I?" George said with a smile.

"I guess not!" Phillip laughed loudly. "Oh, and I got a cat. I called him Grinch because he turns up his nose at everyone, but he liked me enough to follow me home. Mom said I can keep him."

George noticed his family pulling out a board game. "That's great, Phillip. I have to go, though. Let your Mom know I'll called."

"I will, George. Nice talking to you!"

Seven was too many for Life, and Lila offered to sit out.

"It's okay, Lila, Adam and I can share a car." Daphne smiled at her boyfriend next to her. They were less and less separable by the day. George had expected being together at school might put a damper on that, but the opposite had occurred. Adam leaned forward and pecked her lips, making Daphne giggle.

George smiled. It was so good to see her happy again. He couldn't begrudge the time they spent together when it was with the whole family like this, so he stopped, settling back in his chair.

"I don't mind," Lila insisted. "You both should play."

"I kinda like this idea." He popped a blue piece in next to Daphne's pink one.

"You're not married yet!" Janet complained.

George froze. They were getting married. It seemed obvious when said straight, but he hadn't really thought about it before. He still didn't know everything about Adam and how he fit in with what had happened with James and Daphne, except that he'd brought her out. He'd stepped in and paid for it, with blood. George's eye drifted over the scar in Adam's eyebrow. After months of visits, he'd gotten to know Adam. He couldn't think of a better man to marry his little bug. He would look after her, forever.

"Da-ad!" Janet complained now. "Pick!" she laughed and held out the jobs. George plucked one out. "Doctor! You should be a doctor Dad. Then we'd have lots of money."

"Janet," Eva chided.

"What? We would," she said. "I love you, Daddy, no matter what job you have." She rolled her eyes, obviously only trying to appease her mother.

"You have to go to school for years and years to be doctor, silly," Marlene said. "Dad didn't even..." She stopped and turned a little red.

"Finish high school," George finished for her. "It's true. I dropped out in ninth grade." He grinned at his daughter. "And what grade are you in?"

"Nine," she said sheepishly. "Why didn't you finish, Dad?" She took her turn and spun the wheel.

George shrugged. "It wasn't as important when I was your age. I knew enough to add the lengths and cut the board, or divide in half and thirds to make equal pieces. That was all I needed." He spun for himself and picked up a wife, kissing Eva.

He looked at Daphne now. "You'll be the first Kingston to finish school, you know," he told her. She looked down at her hands, then smiled shyly. "I'm proud of you. All of you," he let his eyes rest on each girl, finishing with Lila. She seemed startled. "Especially you, Lila."

"But she isn't going to school!" Janet said hotly.

"No. Do you know why?" he asked her.

Janet shifted in her chair. "Because she's going to have a baby."

"That's right. It's not going to be easy for her. I'm proud of her for choosing to come here, share her baby with us."

Lila's green eyes went wider and filled with tears.

"I'm proud of you," he said again, fiercely, "for making a good choice, for accepting what you have and what you're given, for being the woman you are."

"She's not a woman," Janet said with a pout. Marlene chuckled and eventually the rest of the table joined in.

"Well, young woman."

After the game, George called Kingman again.

"Hello?"

"Mae?" he asked this time, but he was fairly sure it wasn't Cindy.

"Yes. This is she."

"It's George ... Kingston. You helped me find the Spencers a few months back."

"Oh! That George," she said in much the same tone as her son. "Phillip just said George had called before I stuffed him in bed. How are you?"

"Not bad."

"You ever find him?" she asked and he heard a grinding rasp before a sharp intake of breath, lighting a cigarette.

"No," George said softly. "I found another girl instead."

"I didn't take you for that kind of man, George," she said, exhaling.

He chuckled and shook his head. "You know I don't mean that." He cleared his throat, suddenly uncomfortable. "I was wondering if there was anyone new in town."

Mae inhaled and exhaled before answering. "You know I'm not a friend of the Spencers."

George was quiet for a while, not sure what to say.

After another long drag on her cigarette Mae said, "I have seen a new person around their house."

George sighed. "Thank you, Mae. Just the one?"

"Yep, young man, blond, built like a shithouse." She blew out another lungful of smoke. "He the one you're looking for?"

"Nope. That's his brother, Harry. Thanks, though, for keeping an eye out." George felt bad now about calling. "I heard you picked up a better shift at the diner."

"Yeah. Days. It's good. I'm also getting more hours. Still see Ron from time to time."

George chuckled. "And how's he doing?" It had been a week or two since he'd gotten a call from Ron.

"He's good. Still trying to grab my ass when I'm not fast enough. Good thing I'm fast," she said with a laugh.

George laughed too. "He's a good guy. Gave me a place to stay when I was in Knoxville."

"Is that right? You were in Knoxville?"

"Yeah, actually found the creep there, but he got away. That's where I found Lila," he said with a sigh.

"Lila," Mae echoed. "Like your daughter?"

George sighed again. "Unfortunately and worse. She's pregnant."

"Son of snake," Mae cursed. "How old is she?"

"Sixteen."

"Fuck. Excuse my language, George, but my ex got me knocked up nearly that young. It's no life for a girl."

"It won't be. She's with us now," he said proudly. "We'll make sure she gets the life she should have had."

He heard Mae take another drag. "You're a good man, George."

"So is Ron," he put in.

"Yeah, I suppose he is," she said grudgingly.

"It's getting late though. Thanks for checking up for me. I really appreciate that."

She snorted and then coughed. "Because Kingman is so big. It's nothing, George, really. If another Spencer turns up, I'll let you know."

"I'd appreciate that Mae, thank you."

"And next time you talk to Ron, tell him to keep his hands to himself."

George laughed. "I will, Mae. I will. Good night."

Eva was standing in the stairwell, watching him. "Who was that?"

"Remember the waitress in Kingman I told you about?"

Eva nodded. "Yes. Anything?"

"No, just Harry," George grumbled.

"I thought you were going to let the police handle this? You have more than enough on your plate with what's already in this house." She gave him a level look, daring him to argue.

"You're right. Maybe I'll ask at the department, though. Just make sure they're still looking."

"George," she said chidingly. He came over and hooked an arm around her waist, kissing her.

"Just a check in, that's all." He could let it go if he knew someone was picking the ball up, but he had to be sure. "Really. Twenty minutes at the station and I'm done. Can we go to bed now?" he asked, gazing into her blue eyes.

"Okay," she said reluctantly. "Come on, then."

He stopped for a moment outside Daphne and Lila's door, hearing them whispering. He smiled, hoping they each found strength in the other.

***

"What time do you get off?"

Patty's head came up from the tumbler she was topping with cola. Smirking, she slid a cardboard square with the drink to Rudy in exchange for his bill. Rudy hadn't spoken, though he muttered thanks before lifting the glass to his lips.

The speaker was a tall man with straight, dirty-ash hair. A little lighter, a little curlier, and he'd look like James.

"What can I get you?" she asked rather than answer his question. Her wide lapels left a deep neckline that the stranger's eye dove into as she faced him. Patty rolled her eyes. There wasn't much to see there. Starving herself had left her with little to nothing in the way of breasts.

"Bud," he declared loudly, making himself heard over the music. She nodded and bent to pull out the bottle. Those eyes were still on her, little surprise there. Cracking off the cap, she slid it over the plastic coated top of the bar. It coasted easily into his hand.

"You have anything on you?" she asked, crossing her arms on the bar and letting him lose his eyes in her collar again.

"I ... I have some weed," he mumbled.

She sighed and pushed back. Waylon spotted her then and stepped in. "She's not using. You just back off."

The man lifted his hands in surrender. "I didn't mean ... I don't have ... I was just asking."

Patty chuckled and patted her boss on the shoulder. "Easy. He was only offering a joint."

"Oh," Waylon said, a little surprised. "Well, you could take a break, Patty. I've got the bar." His smile was fond now, eyes darting from the man to herself.

"No, thank you," she answered politely.

"Yeah, sure, okay." The stranger took several long pulls from the bottle before lighting up the hand-rolled marijuana.

Sighing, she leaned on the bar and took the smoke from his hand. "What's your name? I really don't care for this stuff," she muttered, dragging the smoke into her lungs. Exhaling from the side of her mouth she turned it back around to him. "I usually need something to pick me up, not mellow me out."

His smile was warm, though he dragged his hand through his hair as though still nervous. "Neil," he answered. "I find I'm too wound up. This is perfect for me." He took another drag, chasing it with a swig from the bottle. "My sister made me brownies once. That was the best afternoon ever." His eyes lost focus a bit. They weren't blue, Patty noticed as they did. They were brown, much warmer than Nancy's or James'.

She didn't know what to say, so went back to her job, fetching the school janitor, Rudy, another rye. Neil stayed where he was, watching her as Rudy was replaced with regular after regular. She'd learned all their names, listened to all their complaints. Neil was not a regular; Patty didn't think she'd ever seen him before. Every time her tasks brought her to his part of the bar, though, he looked up and smiled.

In the early hour, she took the empty bottle from him to stack with the others. The quiet seemed thicker for the music that had kept conversation at bay. "Good night," she murmured. Jumping a little, she gasped when his hand seized out to take hers, still around the bottle.

Reflexively, she gripped the bottle tightly, and reached for another beneath the bar. She could break it use it for a weapon.

"Can I walk you home?" he asked, eyes boring into hers.

In shock, she released the bottle she had started to grab as well as the one on the bar. The empty fell and rolled away. "Uh ... sure, I guess." Recovering a little, she asked, "Do you know how I charge?" Stretching along the bar she grabbed the bottle, not flinching when Neil's hand brushed hers to reach it first.

"Charge?" he asked, brow crinkling. "Oh ..." The look of disappointment stabbed at Patty, though she wasn't sure why. She put the bottle away, giving him time to leave. He held a wad of bills, mostly ones and fives when she turned back.

He didn't know. Her brow creased now. "You ... what do you want?" she asked, covering his hand to stop the counting.

"Uh ... dinner? A movie?" He blushed. Had Patty ever see a man blush before? It still made no sense.

"I don't think I'm the person you want," she answered, pulling her leather jacket on and turning off lights. He followed her to the door, opening it for her.

"Let me decide that," he said, smiling.

She shook her head as she locked up. She knew what he would decide.

A week later with no calls from Neil, she was proven right.

Chapter Sixteen

Lila felt huge. She wasn't actually that much bigger, she supposed, but the little bump protruded significantly. Doctor Gray didn't seem concerned, saying her development was proceeding normally.

She continued to visit Mrs. Peterson, Wanda, she reminded herself, weekly. She couldn't drink the tea anymore; it made her have to pee so quickly.

"Good afternoon, Lila," Wanda said as she came in for her sixth visit. She wore a red cardigan over a white blouse. After adjusting her glasses, she poured herself a cup of tea. There was a pitcher of water on the coffee table.

"Thank you," Lila said with a smile, pouring herself a glass.

"I never had any children myself, but I remember what my sisters went through. How are you feeling?"

"Huge," Lila complained, slouching back on the couch. "I know I'm supposed to get a lot bigger, but I feel so big now!"

Wanda laughed and Lila supposed she still wasn't two-thirds as large as the other woman. She sipped her water. There was an odd fluttering and a thump inside her. Her brow furrowed.

"Something wrong?" Wanda asked.

"I ..." it came again, a small thump. She put her hand to her belly. "I think he just kicked."

"Bless you, child! That's wonderful!" Wanda jumped up to hug Lila.

Lila shuddered a little with emotion and then let the larger woman go, holding herself again.

"Congratulations, dear. I'm happy for you. Well! That was exciting!" Wanda seemed to need a moment to collect herself, adjusting her cardigan and glasses before patting her hair. "What do you think your sisters will say?"

Lila smiled broadly. Her sisters. And they were. Not even two months past, but she knew Janet or Marlene would treat her just the same as they did Daphne. She almost wished Janet wouldn't. That girl could talk forever.

"I think Daphne won't say anything but smile a lot." Wanda chuckled into her teacup and nodded. "Marlene will say something like you did; congratulations, and how exciting it is. And Janet ..." Lila cast her eyes around the room. "She'll probably demand I do something to make him kick so she can feel it."

Wanda laughed. "Really? Daphne doesn't talk of Janet much these days."

"Really," Lila said, rolling her eyes. She sat back and smiled, thinking of her sisters.

"You've changed, Lila. Even in just a month."

Lila sat a little straighter. "I don't know what you mean."

"Tell me about James," Wanda said seriously, all humor and familiarity gone.

"We've talked about James," Lila said, sipping her water.

"You've told me he's the father. That he picked you rather than you him. But you haven't told me about him. What was he like? How did he make you feel?"

Lila licked her lips. "He was everything," she said. "Everywhere. At any time, I could turn and he might be there, just out of sight."

"Did you like that? How did knowing he was there make you feel?" Wanda encouraged, trying to draw the words out of Lila.

"Watched."

Wanda sighed a little and sipped her tea again. Lila noticed that for the first time she held her notepad during the session. "Did that make you uneasy?"

"Sometimes," Lila admitted. "Sometimes it scared me, knowing he knew where I was, what I did or didn't do. Sometimes it made me feel safe." Looking at the water in her glass, she swirled it.

"And how do you feel now, knowing he isn't watching?" Wanda asked.

"Better," Lila said smiling. "This is better."

Wanda smiled back. "I can tell. So, now that you know this is better, what have you learned? Why is this better?"

Lila didn't know the answer to that. Not really. "Because I have a real family." She had told Wanda about the distance she felt from her parents and brother. "A family that loves me. Couldn't I have them and James too?" she asked, though she hadn't intended to voice the thought aloud.

"A good question. What do you think?"

Lila licked her lips and looked into her water again. James. He had been the center of her world when he was in it. Everything was done for him or with him. Could she have that and the new family?

"No," she said finally. "James took too much of my time, my attention. I wouldn't be able to love my family the way I do." She raised her eyes to Wanda.

She sipped from the cup at her lips, her eyes crinkling at the corners. "Changed," she murmured. "I still want more about James. He took your time and attention, how? Just by his presence?" She set the cup in its saucer.

"No. He ... he taught me."

"You said that before. What did he teach you, Lila? What did he fill your time with?"

Closing her eyes and taking a deep breath she breathed out, "Sex."

"Did you have any experience before he taught you?" she asked, breaking the strain Lila was feeling.

"No, none. I hadn't even started my period."

"Had you ever masturbated?"

Lila stared at her. "I don't know that word."

"Touched yourself, for pleasure." This was a different Wanda. She wasn't hard or cold, but she was ... more intent.

"Oh, no," she said with distaste.

"You don't like to think of that. Why?"

Lila recalled her conversation with Marlene. "Because it's dirty."

"Who told you it was dirty?" Wanda leaned forward on her knees now, holding Lila's gaze.

"Mother. Father. The Vicar ..." she murmured.

"So, you didn't touch yourself until James told you to. Why was it okay then?"

Again, she thought of Marlene. No one had told her to do that, so he could watch. She just ... did. Lila wondered why it hadn't been like that for her.

"Why didn't I?" she asked. "Marlene did. No one told her, and she knew it was dirty, or that people thought it was," she amended. Lila wasn't certain it was such a bad thing anymore.

"Do you have any ideas?" Wanda asked.

Lila shook her head, eyes wide.

"How about because you weren't ready?" she suggested. "Or because you didn't want to?"

Lila nodded.

"Now answer my question, Lila, why was it okay when James told you to touch yourself?"

Lila held her breath. "Because he'd hurt me if I didn't."

"Do you think your family would hurt you because you didn't do something they asked?" Wanda asked. She wasn't referring to the Everetts, there the answer was yes. The Kingstons, though ...

"No. They would never hurt me. No matter what I did, or didn't do." Lila's voice was quiet. "They love me." It was a breath with a few sounds, barely audible. Lila felt tears again. "He didn't love me, did he? He just made me what he wanted, the same way my mom did." Lila covered her face with her hands, sobbing.

She toppled a little as Wanda's weight fell on the sofa beside her. She pulled Lila to her, hugging her.

"You know love now, Lila. Unconditional love. It doesn't mean he didn't love you, but he didn't love you enough. And he certainly didn't love you in the right way."

Lila nodded, thinking about Adam and Daphne. She'd seen what her sister had, how patient he was when she wasn't ready for what he offered. How he was always careful with her, like a wild animal, afraid he'd scare her away. That was how James should have loved her, letting her come to him, instead of chasing her down.

Her tears stopped suddenly and she looked up at Wanda. The older woman's blue eyes were soft and full of pain. Sympathy.

"It's all right, Wanda. I understand now."

Wanda patted her shoulder. "You understand the beginning, dear. We still have a ways to go."

Lila shook her head, and just then another kick came from her baby. She giggled, almost hysterically and put her hand to her belly.

"May I?" Wanda asked, stretching out a hand.

Lila grabbed it and placed it where her own had been. A moment later, another kick came.

"Amazing," Wanda murmured.

Lila nodded in agreement.

***

Lila held her apron to her as she leaned over the table, setting the corn in place. Her belly brushed the table.

"Look at you!" Adam said as he entered the dining room. He, like so many others, touched the protrusion as he kissed Lila's cheek. "You look good."

She smiled. Unlike most people, she didn't mind Adam touching. The ladies at the market though ... She wouldn't have minded a little less attention.

Eva put the last dish on as Lila slid in on Adam's right. Daphne sat across from her, taking Adam's hand. He raised the pair and kissed the back of Daphne's hand.

Lila smiled and looked away. Since she had realized James didn't love her, she was becoming more and more envious of Daphne and Adam. She was happy for them, truly, but wanted the same for herself. One day, she told herself, after the baby.

Looking down the table, her eyes caught George's and his mouth twitched. Something was amusing him.

As plates emptied, Lila felt the baby kicking. "Excuse me," she groaned, needing the toilet, again.

"Just a minute, Lila," Adam said rising. "I'd like everyone here for this."

Confused, Lila sat back down.

Adam rose, still holding Daphne's hand. He dropped it to round the table. Eva was shifting in her seat now. She knew what was happening. Looking at Marlene and Janet, she found expressions of puzzlement, no doubt reflecting her own.

Adam went down on one knee, and Lila gasped, her hand going to her mouth. Daphne was startled, too, but she seemed to almost bounce in her chair.

"What?" Janet asked, looking to Lila. "What's-"

"Daphne, you are my world. You make my life worth living. Please share my world and life forever." Adam cringed, as though regretting the words, but he forged ahead. "Will you marry me?"

"Yes, Adam," Daphne said as soon as he finished. "Without you, I'm not sure I'd be alive. I know I wouldn't be who I am. I would be honored to be your wife."

Adam surged upward, seizing her from her seat and swinging her in a circle.

"Where's the ring, boy?" George asked, chuckling.

"Right," Adam muttered, shaking his head. "Stuffy lines, forget the ring, don't know why she said yes ..."

Lila hid a smile and Daphne actually giggled. She hugged him, trapping the arm that was fishing in his pocket.

"Because you said them anyway. Because you meant them." She released him only to take hold of his cheeks and kiss him. The kiss turned heated, and Lila looked away, feeling herself flushing. Eva and Marlene were also looking away. George's eyebrows knit together for a moment, then he smiled broadly.

Lila turned her head just in time to see Adam slip a gold ring with a solitary diamond onto Daphne's finger.

The urgency of delaying her trip caught up as the baby kicked, hard. "Okay, gotta go." She shuffled out as fast as she could toward the bathroom.

She hurried, and it certainly didn't take much to fill her bladder these days. When she returned to the table, Daphne was in her seat, showing her ring to Janet and Marlene. Eva was on her feet, hugging Adam. George stood behind Daphne, hands on her shoulders.

Lila stood in the doorway for a moment, watching them. Marlene spotted her first.

"Why are you over there? Come see!" She beckoned with a hand and Lila chuckled. Anytime she got the feeling she didn't quite fit into this family, they proved her wrong in moments. Whether it was something as simple and small as being included in an activity or chore, or as large as paying her bills and defending her in front of strangers, Lila was one them.

Rather than join the girls, she went to Eva and Adam, hugging him. "You are so good for her. Will I find a man as good as you?"

Adam patted her back. "Of course you will," he murmured. He backed up suddenly and Lila chuckled. The baby had kicked him. "Fighter are you?" he asked. "Put 'em up." Adam made fists and levelled them with her belly. Eva and Lila laughed together.

***

The squares surrounding Lila were coming together quickly. Eva sat in another chair, stitching.

"Mom?" she said, trying the word out.

Eva's smile was extra bright as she looked up. "Yes?" her voice was a little choked as well. That gave Lila the confidence she needed.

"There's something I'd like to do before the baby is born."

"Of course," Eva said, securing her stitch and setting the hoop aside. "What is it?"

"Would Luke be able to change my name, legally?" Daphne and Adam had laid charges against James and were working with the district attorney, but the family had another lawyer that should be able to do this.

Eva blinked at her a few times. "What were you thinking of changing it to?"

Lila laughed loudly, feeling her belly tighten around the baby. "Lila Kingston!"

"Oh," Eva whispered at first. "Oh!" Lila's new mother came and wrapped her in a hug. "Of course we can do that. You're sure? You want our name?"

Lila nodded, smiling broadly. "Of course I do. One of the last things my mother said to me was that she wouldn't have me ruining her name. I don't want it anymore. I think it is ruining me." Lila paused, letting Eva have moment to digest that. "Plus, you're losing one Kingston, you should have another."

Eva chuckled and hugged Lila. "An excellent point. I'm going to call Luke!" she cheered, jumping up. Lila sat back and rubbed her belly.

"I want you to be a Kingston, too," she murmured. Her baby. James' baby. He wouldn't be like his father, would he? Would the family that adopted him know? Should they? Lila began to worry. Breathing deeply, she wondered if she could keep him after all.

"Lila? Is something wrong?" Eva asked, sitting down next to her. She brushed back Lila's hair, and stroked her cheek and neck.

"I'm worried about the baby," she said, her hand still on her belly.

"Why? Did she stop moving?" Eva put her hands to Lila's belly, too.

"No, Mom," Lila said, shaking her head. "I'm worried about ... who he'll be."

Eva stroked Lila's face again. "You can't control who your children are. You can't make them what you want them to be. You can only lead the way. She'll be fine, Lila. She isn't you, and she isn't him. She is herself, and she'll prove it to you in the first few weeks, I promise," Eva said with a chuckle.

Lila smiled and hugged her new mother a little longer. "Will I be as good a Mom as you?" she asked, thinking she already knew the answer.

"Of course. We'll help you," Eva added, sensing Lila's disbelief. "Every parent has to learn. None of us knows when we start."

"I'm still not ... I don't think I can ... I'm not sure I can keep him," Lila finally managed, choking up.

"Oh, sweetheart. You have another couple months to think about it, but if you want to give her up, we'll understand." She continued to hug Lila, rubbing her arm now.

After enjoying her mom's hug for a while, Lila had to ask, "Why do you call her 'she'?"

Eva shrugged. "Mine were all girls."

Lila laughed.

***

Daphne slid around Lila, climbing under the covers. Lila knew she was being careful in case Lila was asleep.

"I'm awake," she whispered in the dark.

"Oh," Daphne murmured.

Lila needed the outside of the bed now; she was up and down often in the night, usually to the washroom. At least the baby had grown still for a while. She'd noticed that he seemed to wake up just when she wanted to sleep.

The baby might be a girl. Lila didn't know why she thought of him as a he, except that she'd started that way. Eva thought it was a girl. They'd find out in a few weeks. She was so big that sleep was short and elusive, part of the reason Daphne took care.

Lila smiled, remembering the dress Daphne had chosen. The wedding wasn't for several months yet, in August, but Daphne and Eva were already planning. Lila, Marlene and Janet kept out of their way for the most part.

Groaning, Lila tried to roll a little onto her side, but the baby kept kicking away.

"I'm jealous of you," Daphne whispered.

Lila's eyes widened in the dark. "What? Why? I'm jealous of you and Adam!" Her voice was incredulous, but hushed.

"You're going to have a baby," she said even more quietly.

"Yes, and so will you. After you finish school, after you're married, when it makes more sense than this." Lila patted her belly.

Daphne sucked in a breath. "We can't."

"Why not?" Lila asked. "I mean, it's gotten better, right?" They had talked about how each step she and Adam took together was slow, plodding, like breaking down a wall of its own.

"Yes, we ..." she giggled nervously, "we did it, Lila. Saturday, remember?" Daphne and Adam had taken a picnic out into the cold.

"You did? Where?!" The picnic had seemed an odd idea.

"His car," she whispered back. "In the back."

Lila nodded; that made sense. "So ... why can't you have a baby?" she asked. "I mean, you could be pregnant now." She understood that so much better now.

Daphne made a noise in her throat and shook her head. "James ... he hurt Adam, Lila. Don't tell anyone. Only his parents and I know that he can't ..." She didn't finish.

Lila's eyes went wide in astonishment. "But you ... he ... I don't understand," she relented. "Was it ... hard?"

Daphne giggled. "Yes, nice and hard."

Lila rolled her eyes and groaned. "That's not what I meant!" she complained.

Daphne's chuckle faded. "I know. It's not that, it's ... beneath. Although, that is scarred up a bit. I guess it doesn't feel as good as it would before." Daphne's voice dipped a little lower, "He says it's good enough." She snickered, and Lila laughed, too.

With a sigh, Daphne curled into Lila's side. "I love you, Lila. You're my best sister." She yawned.

Lila chuckled again. "Best sister," she whispered to the room; Daphne was already asleep. She had given Lila something to think about. She could give her baby to a couple like Daphne and Adam, one who didn't have a baby of their own. Surely he would find a family as good as hers.

Twisting again, she kissed Daphne's head. "I would give you my baby," she murmured, finally drifting off.

Chapter Seventeen

The paper on the bar wasn't hers. Waylon bought one everyday though. Not that she couldn't afford the paper. She'd been able to afford a lot of things lately. She still paid for drugs with sex, but her job, and she was actually able to keep it to her delight, let her buy clothes, food, pay Mrs. Baker rent for her basement room. She was actually taking care of herself, somewhat.

The announcement surprised her. She had been sure that once James got his fingers into Daphne Kingston, no man would want her again, just like Patty herself. However, Donald and Beverly Glass were happy to announce the engagement of their son, Adam, to Daphne.

She knew she should be happy for Daphne, but instead her stomach roiled. This time she knew it wasn't hunger. Food had proven cheaper than she expected, at least in the portions she ate. No, this was jealousy. She would never be good enough for any man, not for more than a quick fuck. They were happy to use her for that.

"What's that?" Waylon asked, coming up alongside her. "Oh, classmate?" he asked.

Patty shook her head. "Nope. Don't know her; don't wanna." She pushed the paper away and resumed moving bottles to the shelf of the cooler. Maybe tonight she'd pick up someone. Someone to make her feel something, someone with some money. She'd been using a lot less since working for Waylon, keeping it to days she didn't work, but she craved it now. She longed to shed this dirty feeling that came from looking at the girl that was good enough, the one that was worth something.

Suddenly, a smile spread across her face. Maybe Adam Glass didn't know about James. Maybe his bride hadn't told him. No reason she couldn't share the misery, after all.

***

"Dad?"

George snorted and started, shaking out of his sleep. "Huh? What?"

"Dad?" Lila repeated. He was still getting used to her calling him that, not that he didn't love that she did, almost as much as he loved the piece of paper that said she was a Kingston. She had officially turned sixteen and didn't really need a "legal" guardian, but it was something substantial, making her theirs. "I think I need you to take me to the hospital."

He bolted out of bed. "What? What happened?"

Eva moaned and reached out to where he had been.

"Evie," he called to her.

"No," Lila whispered. "The doctor told me it would take hours. Let her sleep."

"You don't know that," George said, turning away to find pants. He flushed hotly; daughter by blood or not, she didn't need to see him naked.

"No, but I'm pretty sure. I haven't felt many contractions, but when I got up for the bathroom, my water broke."

George nodded, pulling a t-shirt over his head. "All right, I'll let her sleep, but you go write her a note." He raked fingers through his hair and pulled socks from the drawer. The baby was coming. Eva was going to be livid, even if nothing happened until long after she arrived. He wasn't leaving Lila to get her, though. Lila wouldn't have to face this alone.

Lila looped her sack on her shoulder, but George pulled it from her. "I've got that. Here, take my arm."

She used one hand to hold her coat closed over her chest. It didn't fit any longer, but with the weather warming, it didn't seem necessary to get a new one. Her weight was heavy on his arm as she leaned into him, balancing on the slippery steps. She sighed when she reached the bottom and made her way to the truck. The step looked impossible for her.

"Here." He put his knee out, giving her another board to rise up.

It took restraint, but George didn't race for the hospital. Lila waited for him to come around and help her down again. She held his hand a little more tightly as they walked through the doors. At the nurse's station, she gave her name.

"Lila Kingston. Wrist please?" A bracelet was secured to her as the nurse asked her a number of questions; when had she gone to the washroom last, when was her last contraction, how much pain was she in. Lila's unease melted away. George stayed until the nurse took her to a room.

"I'm going to ask you to change into this and check your dilation." She held out a gown that tied in back.

"I'll be back as soon as I move the truck," George told her. Lila nodded, taking the gown.

After racing back up the stairs, George found Lila standing in a hospital robe and her slippers. She was partway to the door.

"They say it'll be a while yet, and that I should walk."

George nodded. He remembered keeping Eva calm and active as she worked toward the faster and harder contractions, fearful the whole time. "I'll walk with you."

"Dad," Lila murmured after the third contraction in an hour. "Thank you for trying to find James. Thank you for finding me."

George stiffened for a minute, and Lila's arms wrapped around his chest, hugging him. He slid his around her waist, feeling her baby pressed into him. What would have happened to her if he hadn't come? What would he have done without her? How would she have made her way? How terrible would he feel if he ever found out what their lack of action had caused? Would Daphne be doing as well? He knew the two talked. Would Daphne have been ready to accept Adam's proposal?

"You don't know how glad I am that I did." Tears choked his throat and voice. "I love you, Lila."

"I know, Dad. I love you too. I'm scared," she admitted in a quiet voice. "I mean, the contractions are starting to hurt, and it's going to get worse, isn't it?"

George squeezed Lila's hand as she pulled back slightly. "Yes, sweetheart, it will hurt a lot, but I will be here with you. And your Mom and sisters will be here, too." Daphne, at least, would skip class for this. Eva would likely make sure the younger two attended. Trying to distract Lila, he asked, "Are you going to be ready for school come fall?"

She smiled but kept her eyes on her feet. "I couldn't say right now. I think so." She lifted her head a little, looking at the nurses that were scurrying through the halls. They stopped as one.

"Lila!" Janet shouted. She and Marlene both came running down the hall, hugging their sister. "Does it hurt? How much longer?"

"Janet," Daphne hissed through her teeth, "back off." She shook her head.

Marlene was much more sedate. "Are you scared?" she asked into Lila's ear. Lila nodded. George put his arm around Lila, rubbing her shoulder.

"I'll be okay. This isn't the first baby to be born." Lila took a deep breath, smiling after.

Eva and Daphne swept in next, pushing George out of the way somewhat. He stepped aside to give the ladies room.

Janet's eyes went wide as Lila doubled up with another contraction. Daphne held Lila's hand tightly, murmuring encouragement. Eva turned to George, letting Marlene take Lila's other hand. Janet went to her parents.

"When did they check her last?" Eva asked.

"Is she going to be okay?" Janet asked, concerned.

Eva hugged the youngest girl's shoulder, chuckling. "She's going to be fine."

"Two hours ago, and she wasn't halfway yet. Three sem-i-tars."

"Centimeters," Daphne said from beside them. "How far?" she asked.

"Ten," Eva answered. "The baby isn't coming quickly. I want you girls to go to school."

"Mo-om," Janet whined. Marlene was only a little quieter.

"Lila?" one of the nurses asked. "I'd like to take a fetal heart rate and check your progress."

Lila nodded and the family followed her back to her room, although only Eva and George came through the door with her. George stood to the side while Eva rounded with the nurse.

"Oh!" Eva murmured. "You're much further along now, Lila."

The nurse nodded. "Eight. How are you, Lila? Do you need something for the pain?"

Lila nodded. She hadn't shown more than a cringe or a huff. He wouldn't have known the pain had been worsening at all. George was proud of her as always. The nurse went to find a doctor to administer an epidural. As she was leaving, Lila suffered another contraction, longer and harder than the previous.

"We can stay?" Marlene asked, poking her head in the door as the nurse left.

"Yes," Eva relented, "but not here. The nurse and doctor will need room."

The girls pouted but didn't argue. They shuffled out after dashing in to give Lila quick hugs. George moved to follow.

"Dad?" Lila called. He stopped, turning back to her. "Come back, please?"

He nodded, kissing her forehead. "Of course. I'll trade off with Daphne," he nodded to his eldest daughter, and she smiled back.

In the waiting room, the younger girls had found a Scrabble board and were playing. George settled into a chair and felt the early morning catch up to him.

"George," Eva said, shaking his shoulder.

"Dad!" Janet shouted, and he started awake.

"She wants you," Eva said, kissing his cheek.

George rose, stretching and working out the numbness in some of his limbs. Once on his feet, he hurried to Lila's room, surprised Eva had left and Daphne had stayed.

Daphne held Lila's hand and moved a cloth over her forehead. Lila's red curls were damp with sweat and lank around her face though her smile was beaming.

George hurried to her other side, looking to the nurse and doctor at the foot of the bed. "What should I do?"

The nurse smiled. "Just encourage her to push when it's time."

George's eyes went wide. Why was he here? "Don't you want your mom?" he asked Lila.

She shook her head. "No. I ... want you." She squeezed his hand as another contraction gripped her. "It's so strange, like I can feel it, but I can't."

"Okay, Lila," Doctor Gray said, his hands between her knees. "You're fully dilated. On the next contraction, I want you to push. Can you do that?"

She nodded not answering as the contraction came. She dug her nails into Daphne and George's hands, face turning red with effort, grunting and panting for breath when she stopped.

"That's good, Lila," the nurse said.

"You're strong, Lila. You can do this," Daphne told her.

"You can do it, Lila," he murmured, brushing her cheek, wiping away beads of sweat.

She nodded and gritted her teeth as another contraction came, pushing as hard as before. George grunted himself at her effort, her grip. Her face was so red; he worried about her.

"That's it. The baby's crowning. Just a few more pushes, Lila," the doctor urged.

George held his breath as Lila did, though Daphne cooed to her, chanting. "Push, good. Push, Lila, push."

"That's the head," the nurse said triumphantly. "Next is the shoulders, then it's over, Lila. You can do it."

And she did. Hearing that piercing baby wail, George had never been more proud of her. In fact, he felt a little feeble next to her, all that she had endured, the brave face she held.

"It's a boy." Doctor Gray held a red streaked infant to the nurse who took him in a towel. While the doctor continued to work with the contractions to ease out the afterbirth, the nurse wiped the baby clean. She fixed a tag around his ankle that matched the one on Lila's wrist and then handed the baby to George. He was startled, but closer to the foot of the bed than Daphne. The nurse tied and cut the cord as George held him. The baby was quieter, wrapped up, and his eyes blinked heavily, the deep blue of a newborn. George kissed his head.

"A boy?" Lila asked weakly.

"Yes," Daphne told her. "Dad's holding him. He's beautiful, Lila."

"Go on," the nurse said once she'd finished, and George laid his grandson in Lila's arms.

"I'm so proud of you," he told her, kissing both Lila's and the baby's head. Then he stepped away, taking Daphne's hand as she rounded the bed. Eva and the girls had just returned.

"I'm proud of you, too," he said kissing her temple.

"I didn't do anything," she complained, looking very disheartened, more so than he had expected.

"You were there for her. You didn't give up and didn't let her give up. One day it will be your turn." He hugged her again. Was she crying, he wondered. Why?

Chapter Eighteen

Looking at the infant in her arms, Lila ceased to notice anything else in the hospital room. She paid no mind to the doctor still between her legs or to her sisters squealing around her. All her attention was on the large pair of blue eyes looking at her.

He seemed to be wondering what she was. So she answered him, "I'm your mother, but I won't be your Mom." She kissed his head and reveled in his warmth.

Eva kissed the top of her head. "Why not?" she asked.

Shrugging, Lila said, "I'm not ready." Unlike James, this baby couldn't make her do what she wasn't ready for. Especially when she was fairly certain she knew someone who was. "Is Daphne still here?"

"I am," Daphne said coming over.

A nurse came to take the baby. "We need weigh him, and we'll clean him up a little better. Get a diaper on the wee fellow. Isn't that right?" she cooed at the infant.

Lila didn't cling. She wasn't ready to let him go completely, but she knew she had to keep her distance.

"Would you all mind leaving me with Daphne? If you're done, doctor?" she asked, noticing him still bent over a tray.

"Oh, yes, just finished." He stepped up and patted her thigh through the sheet covering it. "You did great, Lila. You and he will both be fine."

"Thank you, Doctor Gray," she said with a smile. The rest of the family filed out, Janet pleading to know what they were naming him. Daphne and Lila both laughed at her.

"Do you know what you want to call him?" Daphne asked.

Shaking her head, Lila told her, "That's something I wanted to talk to you about. You and Adam. I know he's not here, but ... well, you probably know what he'll say. I want you to have him."

Daphne gasped. "We're just finishing High School, Lila. I don't think we're ready to have a baby, either."

"I know," Lila argued. "Mom and I can watch the baby during the day, but he'll be your son, living with you and Adam."

"I can't accept this, Lila. He's yours. I can't take him from you." Her brown eyes were sad, desperately wanting what she offered. Lila wondered if she really wasn't ready.

She looked away. "He'll be taken from me anyway. I would rather he went to you," she whispered, voice thick with emotion.

Daphne sniffled. "I ... I need to talk to Adam. I don't know ... I want to say yes, Lila, you know I do, and you know why."

Lila nodded, clutching her sister's hands. "And that's exactly why I want you to have him. I know you'll raise him well. I'll still be part of his family, too. It would be the best for everyone." Her green eyes locked on brown, begging them to see what she saw.

Daphne sighed heavily. "I can't say yes yet. I will talk to Adam, though." With a small smile she added, "I'm not saying no!"

Lila grinned, giggling slightly. "Right. Talk to Mom and Dad, too. They want me to keep him. I'm sure they'll help you and Adam if you need it."

Daphne nodded, turning. "You're right. I will. Rest, Lila. It's been a long day for you already."

Stopping, she turned back to the bed and kissed her sister's forehead. "Justin," Daphne murmured. "I think we should call him, Justin."

Lila nodded, liking that. Then she closed her eyes and fell asleep.

When she woke, her bed had moved. Not entirely unexpected in a hospital where the beds had wheels. What was strange was the throbbing in her chest. Her breasts hadn't hurt this much when James first grabbed them. She looked down to see wet spots where they had leaked onto her gown. Next to her, in a bassinet was Justin Kingston. She smiled and stood carefully, testing the epidural was completely out of her system, and lifted him out. He wasn't asleep and his mouth seemed to open and close.

A nurse popped her head in. "Ah, I sent them away to let you sleep. Would you like your mother or sister?"

"Yes," Lila answered quickly. "Both." Reaching behind her neck, she pulled the string tying her gown closed. She slipped it off one arm and adjusted the baby, just before her family came in.

"Dad's sleeping," Daphne said, smiling.

"You're going to nurse?" her mom asked. She had seen Lila learn to hold a baby in pre-natal classes. Lila still felt tentative, afraid of hurting Justin. She was even more nervous being watched. "Go on," Eva encouraged. "You've got him just right."

Sighing with relief, Lila took her nipple between her fingers and put it to the baby's lips. He tried a few times, unsuccessfully, to latch on.

Eva chuckled, but didn't seem concerned, so Lila wasn't either.

"Practice?" Daphne asked their Mom.

"Yes. He needs to learn how, that's all. There he goes!" Lila gasped at the sudden tug on her breast, the sensation of something pulling out. She stared down in wonder as the little mouth worked.

Daphne covered her mouth with both hands and giggled. "He's amazing!" she said, bouncing on her toes. "Do you mind if Adam comes in? I mean," she gestured to Lila's chest.

Lila laughed, knocking Justin's mouth free. "Oh, sorry, baby," she murmured, popping the nipple back in his mouth. "No, it's fine, Daphne."

"Thanks." She ran out of the room.

"You know, nursing makes it less likely you'll be able to let him go," Eva warned her.

Looking at the bundle in her arms, Lila answered, "I know. I'm hoping to keep him close." Her Mom nodded in understanding.

Daphne was tugging on Adam's hand. "She said it's okay, Adam, come on!" With a final pull, he stumbled through the doorway and turned away pink-cheeked upon seeing her.

Justin had just let go again, so Lila pulled the gown back up. "It's fine, Adam, I'm covered."

He let out a loud sigh and came closer. One of his hands rested just off the baby's head, over the faint pale hair that was practically invisible. "He's beautiful, Lila."

"Would you like to hold him?" she asked, holding Justin out.

Adam's hands went up, seemingly in surrender, but Daphne put her arms out, taking the bundle. "The nurses let us hold him after the weighing, since you were asleep," she said, pulling him close. "Didn't they, little man? Sure. They thought you might like to get to know your family." It wasn't quite baby-talk, but Daphne's voice, normally soft, was even lighter now. Justin lulled in her bouncing hold, eyes closing.

Lila knew she'd been right to make the offer. Doubly so as she watched Daphne tuck Justin into Adam's rigid arms. He looked scared to death, sitting stiffly in the chair that Eva had suggested would help. Slowly, very slowly, as a nurse took Lila's pulse and blood pressure, Adam relaxed with the baby still in his arms.

"I ... Excuse me," Lila said rising. She needed the toilet and was dreading it. Her bottom still throbbed all along her sex. She had to do it though, her prenatal classes had taught her that, too.

With relief, the dreaded moment passed with barely any pain. She flushed happily. "Has Justin filled a diaper yet?" she asked as she emerged.

"Nope, just wet so far," Eva answered. Justin yawned widely in Adam's arms and opened his blue eyes, gazing up at the face of the one who held him.

"Um ... Hi?" Adam made it a question rather than greeting. Lila shared a look with Daphne; they both thought the exchange adorable and a little ridiculous.

The baby's mouth opened and closed a few times and he stretched out with a hand. Adam started, going rigid again, but Justin's fist curved in and landed in his mouth. His lips closed on it and started sucking.

"Whoa," Adam murmured, completely awestruck.

Lila stepped up and took the baby in her arms again. "He's still hungry," she explained, "and you won't get any milk out of that," she told Justin, pulling the fist away. He made an angry face and let out a single cry.

"Aw," Daphne cooed, watching his nose and forehead scrunch as he worked up to a second cry. Before he managed, Lila pulled down the other sleeve and got him latched on the other breast.

Adam looked away at first, but eventually was drawn back to the baby in her arms. "Does that hurt?" he asked.

Eva and Lila both chuckled. "No, not really. Odd, for sure." Lila explained. She shifted, thinking about a man doing what this baby was. Giving Adam a small glare, she returned her attention to Justin. "It's kinda nice. It takes the pressure off anyway," she said with sigh, noticing that the one didn't pain her nearly as badly any longer. The milk was building again, though; she could feel it start to pinch toward the nipple. Looking, she noticed the wet spot spreading on that side. She looked to her mom, raising an eyebrow.

"That's normal," she said with a smile. "It'll stop after a week or two. You're just so full right now, it comes out all the time."

"I am," Lila said with a groan. She squeezed the free one and watched the spot spread. Adam turned red again and rose to leave. "Wait," Lila said to stop him. "Did you and Daphne talk at all?"

He looked to Daphne, then back to her. "Yes. We're going to talk to my family, too, but I like your idea. I think we'll find a way."

"I can look after him," she offered again, as she had to Daphne.

Daphne shook her head. "No you can't. You start school again in the fall. Hopefully he'll take well to formula. They say it's as good as breast milk or better."

"Should I not feed him?" Lila asked Eva.

She shook her head. "It's what babies have lived on for centuries. I think it will do for Justin."

Lila settled back against her pillows, letting Justin continue to nurse. She sighed with relief. Justin would have a home, have a family, be loved.

***

Lila rose groggily at the infant's wail, but Daphne had already hopped off the edge of the bed, bringing Justin to her. "Here you go," she said slipping her pillow behind Lila's shoulders so she could sit against the headboard.

"Thank you," Lila replied.

Daphne leaned against her, watching the baby. "I don't mind. I love this part."

Lila loved it, too. Justin had grown so much in just a few months. His bassinet sat on top of one of the dressers, but he would need a crib soon.

Adam had found an apartment for himself and Daphne. He was planning to move in at the beginning of July with Daphne joining him after the wedding in August. Until then, Justin would share this room with them. Their lawyer, Luke, had started filing the paperwork for the adoption shortly after Justin's birth, though everything was post-dated for the wedding. He wouldn't be Justin

Kingston, then. He would be Justin Glass the same day Lila's sister became Daphne Glass.

Yawning wide enough to make her jaw crack, Lila turned to said sister. "You should be sleeping. You have exams tomorrow."

"I know. He doesn't feed long." She couldn't take her eyes from her son, their son. For these months, he really did belong to both of them, and it was perfect.

"He's starting to look like James," Daphne mused, running her finger over Justin's brow.

Lila nodded, uncomfortable. "He looks a little like my brother, though. His cheeks," she mused, tapping the one pointed up.

"Good. I wonder if anyone will ever bother him about not being ours." She meant hers and Adam's. Lila felt a twinge for a moment.

Pushing it away, she reminded herself what good parents they would be, while she needed to finish school and grow up a little more herself. "Adam's hair is light enough. I'll bet people say he looks like him."

Daphne nodded, hopeful. Justin passed out again, losing his latch. Daphne took him, settling him back in his bassinet. Lila had slept on the outside the first week home from the hospital, but it was ridiculous when Daphne still beat her to the bassinet half the time. They'd swapped sides at that point.

Adam and Daphne had their last exams in the morning. After that, Daphne would be home with them. Janet and Marlene had to finish the week, and then the house would be hectic. Lila had gotten accustomed to her days alone with Eva. She would miss them. On the other hand, she did love her sisters.

They'd be torn between playing with Justin and wedding planning. Janet would want to play with Justin all day every day. Eva would help keep her from doing so. Marlene wouldn't be nearly as pushy. Also, they were all involved in making favors for the wedding, so there was work to keep them busy.

Lila felt sleep swamp her as soon as her head hit the pillow again. How did Daphne manage to jump up after Justin so easily? Her mind filled with images of a golden haired boy walking between Daphne and Adam.

Chapter Nineteen

George picked up the phone, wondering who was calling so late in the evening. "Hello?"

"George, it's Ron. You'll never guess where I'm calling from."

He rubbed his eyes, looking at the clock. It was eleven and six would come early, especially if Justin had another fitful night. He'd had more and more of those lately. He was so close to making it through the night, waking just before George would normally rise.

"Ummm west, west ... San Francisco?" George guessed.

Ron snorted. "No, much more interesting. I'm at Mae's house!"

"What?!" George asked incredulous. "Did you steal her key or something?"

"No, you ass, she invited me for the night."

"Why?"

"Do I have to draw you a picture?"

George shook his head. "No, why are you calling?"

"Oh, right. It wasn't to gloat. Well, not just to gloat."

George heard Mae's voice in the background. "Are you spreading rumors about my virtue, Ronald?"

"No rumors, just fact," he called back. "Actually, I called 'cause Mae has some news for you. Shit! I forgot it's an hour later there. Sorry, George. I'll get her. Mae! I called George."

George waited and eventually a female voice came on the line. "I can't believe I don't have your number. I had to get it from Ron. Luckily, he was headed this way." He heard a smacking that he was pretty sure had been a kiss.

"This isn't the first night he's spent there, is it?" George asked, chuckling.

"No," Mae said slowly, "but don't let him tell you I was an easy catch. I made him work."

"Damn straight you did!" Ron's voice came through, though muffled.

"Anyways, I needed to call you. I've been keeping an eye on the Spencers. Everyone's been watching the new boy since his record got out." There was a snapping rasp and a sharp inhalation. "Thanks, baby," she murmured, to Ron, George assumed. He shook his head, surprised by that.

"Harry giving you any trouble?" George asked.

"Not a lick," Mae said, exhaling. "He's taken up coaching the little league team. Phil's little league team," she said with emphasis.

George straightened. "Yes?"

"Yes, and he mentioned that his brother was still on the move, not settling down. I commented that it was a hard way to live and told him a bit about Ron. He agreed and told me his brother was currently trying to find a place for himself in Michigan, near the border, although Harry expects he won't stay there long."

George's breath caught. "You have no idea what this means to me, Mae."

"I'm hoping it means enough that you'll invite me to your daughter's wedding, you lout."

George laughed. "You aren't coming with Ron?" he asked.

"I am, but I thought I warranted my own invitation." George could just imagine her pointed nose up in the air.

"Of course you do," he agreed. "I hope you'll bring Cindy and Phillip as well."

"Will do. Ron's telling me it's approaching midnight there. We should let you go. Oh, and just because he is gallivanting across the country all the time, doesn't mean you can't call me once in a while."

George chuckled again. "Point taken. I just figured you didn't need me hassling you."

"You're no hassle, George, and I don't appreciate hearing you're a grandfather through Ron."

He looked at his feet, sheepish. She couldn't see it, but he was sorry he hadn't told her. "Sorry about that. Justin. Was six pounds five ounces, but now he's pushing twenty pounds and can almost roll over!"

She chuckled. "They grow up too fast, don't they? God, I can't even imagine Cindy having one in a few years, though I suppose it could be my turn soon enough." She sighed heavily.

"You could still have another of your own," he reminded her.

"Shit, don't say that. I'm making him cover up. God ... another kid. Ugh." George could hear her shudder.

"What's wrong with having a baby with me?" Ron asked indignantly in the background.

"Yours or anyone else's, I don't want it," she said snidely. "George, let me go and box this man's ears, all right?"

"All right. You take care, Mae." He turned, hanging the phone up and saw Lila, Daphne and Eva in the kitchen.

"Who was that?" Eva asked.

"Yes, who's coming to the wedding?" Daphne asked.

Lila didn't say anything, just smiled, Justin in the crook of her arm. Still, he wondered how they all got there so quietly. He could have sworn he had the room to himself. With light steps, Marlene and Janet looked around the stairwell.

George sighed. "Mae. The waitress in Kingman that helped me find the Spencers there. Harry's coaching her son's little league team," he explained.

Eva's breath caught and she put a hand to her mouth. Lila's eyes went wide and her mouth hung open. Daphne shook her head slowly. The younger girls just raised brows, not understanding.

"Apparently, his brother was in Michigan, but he doesn't expect him to stay there long. I'm going to the station in the morning, let them know."

"You're going with them," Eva murmured.

George met her eyes, glittering hazel. She'd accepted so much for him. "Yes," he said quietly. "If I can be there ... yes."

"Daddy? Who are the Spencers?" Marlene asked. If it had been Janet, he probably would have told her to go to bed, but Marlene would only ask if it was weighing on her mind. He met Daphne's eye, urging her to answer.

"Justin's father," Lila said. "He hurt me and Daphne, and Dad's going to help the police catch him." Her green eyes were full of fire. She wanted this. If she could have come along, George had no doubt she would have.

Daphne nodded. "He hurt Adam, too. That's why we're going to court. We're going to stop him from hurting anyone else."

Marlene nodded, but Janet still looked confused. "I don't remember you being hurt, Daphne. And if he's Justin's dad, how did he hurt you?" she asked Lila.

Silence was heavy in the room. Justin let out a loud burp that brought milk up on his sleeper. Eva took Janet up to the room she shared with Marlene, trying to explain on the way. "Lila didn't want to have a baby, Janet ..."

Marlene got a cloth from the sink and gave it to Lila, who dabbed at the sour milk. Justin smiled showing that first white tooth that had just broken through.

"Yuck it up," Lila told him. "You're the one who's going to be hungry later."

"Marlene, would you mind changing him?" Daphne asked.

"Sure," she said with a smile, taking the baby from Lila. "We'll get you cleaned up, Jay."

Lila closed her eyes and Daphne's hands balled in fists. Even George wasn't without reaction, clenching his jaw hard. Sadly, the nickname was catching on, even though it was too close to James.

"Dad, are you sure you want to go with them?" Daphne asked. "You don't have to. We're ready, the DA and Adam and I. You can let the police do this."

"I intend on letting the police do it. I just need to see him. I need to be there."

"Why? In case he's hurt another girl?" Lila asked.

George's stomach turned. "God, I hope he hasn't. Sounds like he's been moving a lot, so I doubt it. No, I just need to make sure it's done, that's all."

Lila's hands, formerly on her hips, came out to wrap around George, hugging him tightly. "I love you, Daddy. Be careful."

"I will."

He was tackled from the other side as Daphne's arms circled his waist, her head tucked in his side. "Yes, be careful."

He rubbed her back. "I won't be gone long," he promised.

***

Two weeks of following dead leads, two weeks of listening to cops who didn't have time for him. George had given up. He was looking on his own again. He had an entire state to search and apparently the authorities didn't have enough time or resources. He'd been to Ann Arbor and Flint and turned up nothing. In Detroit, he thought he'd found something, a car dealership that had fired a James Spencer. He'd asked around, poked, and gotten snapped at more times than he could count, but finally an old bartender at a hole James frequented said something about Dearborn. It was all the lead he had, but he would take it.

So it was that George found himself driving through Dearborn looking for another lead, another bar, another job. He'd contacted the station here. They had the same APB for James that all of the departments in Michigan had received, and like all the departments George had visited, they had no one to dedicate to the search. He'd spent all of twenty minutes with Detective Oscar Mitchell, telling him what he knew of James, passing over a worn high school photograph. After copying the image, he had passed it back to George and wished him luck.

Focused on driving, George didn't quite believe it when he saw the blond man he only recalled dimly. He did a second and a third take, needing to be sure. Once he realized that the man with Lila his first day in Fort Knox was James, he'd done his best to recall what he could, any changes from the school picture. His coloring was similar to his mother but his curls came from Joshua. He was more slender than Josh, though, broad shoulders but narrow hips. That was all George had to go on besides a yearbook photo. Was it him?

Swerving into the park lane, he threw the brake on and ran from the truck.

James turned his head at the screeching tires and saw George running toward him. He spun and began to run in the other direction. That was confirmation for George. The bastard was fast, probably as fast as Lila. Well, he *was* as fast, George knew that.

Wheeling, George jumped back in the unlocked truck and pulled a u-turn from his space. There were squeals from the tires of other cars, but no crashing. With luck, one of those or the owners of the stores on either side would call him in. James slowed, looking over his shoulder and seeing no one. He walked into the street, not watching his step, and George pulled hard to the left, cutting off traffic again, but he was successful. There was a satisfying thud as he hit the asshole, clipping him with the corner of his steel bumper.

"Fuck! Goddamn! What the hell?" James' string of profanity stopped when George, four-way lights flashing, opened the door of the truck, right on top of him.

"Are you hurt?" he asked with no hint of concern in his voice. George would correct the oversight if necessary.

"Who are you?" James demanded.

"I am a father. *The* father. You hurt my girls, and I'm going to make sure you never hurt another girl again."

That was when the sound George was waiting for came. Sirens rang out behind him. James started to pull himself up, trying to run again. George's boot caught the leg he'd clipped, sending the molester sprawling again on the asphalt.

"Didn't break anything? Pity." His full weight on James' leg made him scream, but kept him in place as the police exited their cruiser.

George's hands were already out and spread. James' were quickly cuffed by one officer while the other did the same to George only slightly more gently.

"Is this necessary? If you want, you can drive me and my truck to the station. Detective Oscar knows who I am."

"Jimmy?" the officer called to his partner. "You got that one?" James was being pressed into the back seat of the cruiser. Jimmy nodded. "I'm going to take this one in his truck. That cool?" Jimmy nodded again, opening the driver's door. "I'm trusting you," the cop warned.

"I know. I'm George Kingston. That's James Spencer."

"Spencer. I know that name. Huh. Well, that won't save you from a ticket for reckless driving."

George nodded. "It'll be my second traffic violation in twenty years," he said with a smile. "Well worth it."

The officer snorted, pulling into the back of the station and opening George's door for him, taking him to a holding cell.

"I'll tell Oscar you're here. I'm sure it won't be long." George nodded to him as he left. Thankfully, they hadn't put him in the same cell as James.

"...slut. Fucking Daphne. If she'd just stayed mine ... I should have killed that kid instead of just ruining him. Mom's gonna kill me."

George breathed deeply through flaring nostrils. Counting, he tried to calm himself and not listen to the drivel James was spouting. It was up to the courts to deal with him now. And if they didn't ...

"George?" Detective Oscar brought him out of his violent thoughts. "Come on upstairs. I need your statement." He nodded and followed the detective. "That wasn't the best way to deal with this, George. You gave me a shitload of paperwork, you know that?"

"Sorry about that. He was just too damn fast."

Oscar nodded. "Yeah, it was a clean hit. Didn't even break the skin. I think we can pass the whole thing as a traffic infraction. It's going to be a steep fine, though, hitting a pedestrian."

George just nodded. "It's worth it. I want him behind bars where he can't hurt any more girls."

Oscar nodded. "A bail will be set, but we'll be able to keep a watch on him."

George sighed with relief. He didn't even blink at the pink slip of paper handed to him on his way out the door.

***

Patty smiled as she pushed her grocery cart to the till. There wasn't more than a bag or two in it, bread, eggs, some fruit and vegetables. She didn't really cook, except to fry eggs. It all seemed tasteless to her, no matter what she did, so she just ate what she needed.

The super-slim model on the cover of Elle drew her eye and she picked it up, her nose in the pages as she pushed in behind the woman unloading her cart.

"George Kingston found him. You heard Harry is out, living with Josh's relatives, but apparently the younger was worse. Sexual assault, of Daphne! I'm so glad he's been gone, and even more glad he's caught. Nancy Spencer might think the world owes her something, but nothing good has ever come from that family."

Hearing Spencer, Patty looked up. She knew neither woman's name, though she'd seen them around town all her life. No doubt they didn't know her name, either. Patty put her things on the counter quietly as the last item purchased by the woman ahead of her was bagged.

"A sex crime, here in Fort Garland. I thought we were too small for such things."

Patty had to snort at that, which drew haughty glares. "Nothing, just ... wondering how many sides a place this small can have."

The woman behind the till nodded slightly. "More than one, apparently." She took the other woman's money and passed her the bags. "Did you want Leo to help you to your car?"

Patty stopped listening again. *The younger one was worse. George Kingston found him. Glad he's caught.* Was James in jail? It didn't seem possible. Had Daphne actually talked to the police? What kind of guts would that take? Patty still couldn't think of it. James would kill her before they got to court, for certain.

"That'll be twenty-two sixty," the woman said, waking Patty from her daze. She handed over a few bills and started digging for change.

"Was that James Spencer you were talking about? He's been arrested?" She passed over her quarters.

"That's right. George Kingston hit him with a truck, if the rumors are true. I think that one can't be." The woman didn't say more and Patty didn't want to draw too much attention to herself, certainly not in connection with James. She was better off without any ties to him.

"Are you finished?" an authoritative voice asked. Patty flinched instinctively, clutching her bag. Then she placed the voice and turned.

Nancy Spencer was behind her, unloading her own cart. She wrinkled her nose at Patty.

"Are you?" she repeated.

Patty smiled. "I am. I hear your second son is joining the first behind bars. Something in the upbringing?" She tugged on her leather jacket, seeking the tenacity to stick this out. The woman at the till took in a sharp breath while Nancy let one out in a huff.

"James has been charged, not convicted. I'm sure the Kingston girl is confused and James' innocence will be proven." Her red lips pulled back from white teeth as she smiled. A predatory smile. Patty snatched up her groceries and headed for the door. Before she opened it though, she turned back once more.

"James hurt Daphne, just like he hurt me, and he will pay." She didn't wait for an answer; she didn't expect one, but even as she said it, she believed. He would pay, and so would Nancy.

Chapter Twenty

The pink dress looked terrible with Lila's red hair. Thankfully, it was such a light pink as to be almost white. She thought it strange that she would wear a color so close to the bride's.

Her mom was fixing Daphne's veil in place, Eva's own veil. Brown curls fell around Daphne's radiant face.

Janet and Marlene were both wearing their best dresses, but the family couldn't afford too many new ones. The one Lila wore belonged to a cousin she had met for the first time yesterday. Daphne's dress was new. Layers of white lace made it light and cool on the hot summer day. Justin was in Marlene's arms, his chubby cheeks pulled back in a grin as she cooed at him.

There was a knock at the door and George came in with the flowers. "Nearly ready?" he asked, looking nervous himself. Daphne's skirt rustled and Eva flipped the veil forward. "You look ready," he mused.

Daphne didn't answer but took the flowers he held out to her. Lila took the smaller bundle, still amazed that she was to be the Maid of Honor.

"Okay, girls, you two should find your seats. We'll be starting right away." Eva kissed Daphne's cheek over the veil and then

Lila's. Marlene and Janet each kissed Daphne and wished her luck as well. Justin tried to grab the veil when it came within his reach.

Lila was glad she'd already swapped him to formula; she really didn't need any leaking today. As an added bonus, her breasts were small enough to fit in the dress. It would have been painful to wear a month ago.

George hugged Daphne. "I'm so happy for you, sweetheart. I'm going to miss having my little bug at home."

"I know, Daddy. We'll only be a few blocks away." Daphne's voice was thick with tears. Lila left the room to give them a moment alone.

Padding down the stairs in her bare toes, she donned the dressy sandals that waited for her at the door. Peeking out, she saw the yard filled with chairs and Adam standing next to his cousin under an arch with the Justice of the Peace. The chairs were a mismatch of folding lawn chairs, dining room chairs borrowed from neighbors, and even a couple of stacking stools. Sadly, expense had been a factor in the preparations, but the guests were happy. The food, which she had helped prepare, was ample for those gathered, and if not fancy, it was tasty. She had sampled a bit too much when assembling salads and side dishes yesterday, including a sliver of the cake which was shaved for icing.

Footsteps behind her made Lila turn. George and Daphne were coming down the stairs. Lila opened the door and stepped out. It should be enough to cue the accordion player. With a grin on her face, Lila walked sedately down the aisle, head high and proud.

Once at the front, she was able to turn and look over the guests. Many lived nearby, though out of town, and had just come in for the day. Lila had met some in the months she'd lived here. Cousins, aunts and uncles that had only learned of her in the last weeks, they had welcomed her more warmly than any of her blood family ever had.

Ron sat next to a slender woman with long, black hair. She was beautiful, and she was kissing Ron? Lila blinked twice but averted her gaze, not wanting to stare. It landed on a thin woman in a leather jacket. Another woman she didn't recognize. Soon all attention turned to the house. George held Daphne's hand on his arm as he walked her down the aisle.

Lila's eyes, like so many of the guests', filled with tears upon hearing Daphne's gentle, quiet voice declaring her love for Adam. Soon after came Lila's actual role in this ceremony, witnessing the signing of the register. Signing Lila Kingston gave her one more swell of pride, and she hugged Daphne as the bride rose from signing her own name.

"First time as Kingston," Lila whispered in her ear. Although it had been her name for a little while, she'd never signed anything.

"And my last," Daphne said, sniffing back tears. "I'm so happy, Lila. I didn't think I'd ever feel this happy again."

"I'm not sure I've ever been this happy," Lila admitted. "Not since I was little." She pulled away from the bride so Adam could lead her back to the arch they had made their vows beneath.

The Justice concluded the ceremony, inviting Adam to kiss the bride. It was a gentle peck that Daphne held for longer than he had intended. He chuckled slightly as she pulled back.

The party after was as casual as the ceremony had been. Lila was introduced to many relations, particularly those of Adam, and friends of both families.

"How's my girl?" Ron asked, hugging her. Lila stiffened for only a moment before relaxing into the hug.

"Good. Getting back to normal."

"How's that?" the raven-haired woman with him asked.

"Lila, here, just had a baby a few months back. The boy over there, Justin. Lila, this is Mae, my fiancée, and her kids, Cindy and Phillip." Ron indicated the boy and girl beside him.

Lila exchanged pleasantries with all of them. Later in the afternoon, as people were eating, she managed to catch Mae alone. "You're going to marry Ron?" she asked, still surprised.

Mae laughed. "I am. Can't quite believe it myself. Hope he's easier to train than my last husband. At least he'll be tracking mud in the house less," she grumbled.

"But ..." Lila had no idea how to say what she thinking. She just couldn't imagine being ... romantic with Ron.

"He's a good man, Lila. When you start seeing with your heart, you stop seeing with your eyes so much. Besides, my last was too pretty and that's part of the reason he's gone." She smirked, and Lila nodded with a little more understanding.

"I see. Well, congratulations."

"And to you! That's one fine little boy there, though I got the impression he was Daphne's," Mae mused.

"He is," Lila answered. "She and Adam adopted him today."

"Ah," Mae said, her eyes brightening. "That makes more sense. What will you do now?"

Lila shrugged. "I'm going to finish high school for sure. Then I'm thinking I might look into becoming a teacher."

George seemed to appear from nowhere. "College?" he asked, surprised.

Lila blushed. They wouldn't be able to afford for her to go to college, but she hoped to get a scholarship with a lot of work in her last two years of school. "I would like to," she said quietly.

Startled, she was suddenly in a tight hug. "Have I told you how proud I am of you?" George's voice was in her ear and his aftershave filled her nose.

Chuckling, she answered, "Yes. Once or twice." Mae chuckled, too, seeming to understand her meaning. "But don't worry about it. I'm sure I can get a scholarship."

George pulled back quickly. "We'll get the money saved. I never dreamed of one of my girls ..." He cleared his throat, suddenly embarrassed by the eyes on them. Lila hugged him again, squeezing fiercely.

"I love you, Dad," she told him. "I can do it because of you."

***

Patty sat wearing something fitting, a floral sundress. Her leather jacket was a little out of place, but she would never stop wearing it. It had been lost and found. She was still lost, but she'd be damned if someone wouldn't find her one day, too. The worn brown leather felt like a thicker skin, protecting her from everyone around her, from their stares, their condemnation. It didn't protect her from herself though, from the vileness she knew she was carrying. Everyone here knew about James and Daphne, but they accepted this union, even her soon-to-be in-laws. The envy continued to poison Patty.

Listening to the whispers around her, she wondered if she might find some sympathy for herself from this family, if she were willing to tell them what James had done to her. All talk seemed to be of a red-head the Kingstons had adopted. Another girl mistreated by the villain Daphne and Adam were laying charges against, the one George had helped catch. The relief she'd had the first time she heard he was behind bars intensified. Then it had been rumor, too, but so many mouths, all saying it with certainty, bolstered her.

Well, at least someone had finally thought to set the cops on him. Would they have cared that he broke her arm when they were both eleven? How about that he had used a car lighter to burn a round scar on her hip? Did they know he had ...

She snapped around as the wedding march began and a tall willowy girl with red hair strode down the aisle. She looked sick in that shade of pink, like she was faintly green. Even so, she was beautiful, far more than Patty herself or Daphne. She could see James salivating to have this girl; she could see Nancy welcoming his new wife. The way she carried herself screamed of money. She had not had a hard childhood like Patty, surviving on what came to one of seven stretching a garbageman's wages. She was thin, but not skinny like Patty. Her eyes flicked to the baby in the lap of a girl at the front, the baby rumor said was hers. Hers and James' unless Patty missed her guess.

James, a father. The idea was appalling. What would he have done to that child? Perhaps treated him like royalty, the way Nancy treated James. He might make sure his child knew he, the baby was dressed in blue, could step on people to get his way, or that he deserved the obedience of everyone. On the other hand, he might bend and break that child the way he had Patty, or Daphne, or this girl.

Patty's eyes were now pinned to the boy, even as she rose with the rest of the guests at Daphne's entrance. The fair-haired baby gave her the impression James was actually here. She decided, looking at that angelic face, as beautiful and disarming as James', she wasn't going to say anything and try to slip away again.

The ceremony was brief and she shook Daphne and Adam's hands. It was a surprise to see the baby in Adam's arms as she made her way out of the yard. James was behind bars. The fact that a tiny replica of him was living with the Kingstons shouldn't bother her. After all, a baby couldn't stop her.

Still, she needed a hit. Even though she hadn't had one in weeks, she needed one now. Waylon would be disappointed, if he found out.

He shouldn't find out.

Chapter Twenty-One

Lila walked beside Marlene, fear prickling her. The extended family had been quick to accept her, but what would the average Junior in high school think? Also, she was a year behind. She didn't think that would be what drew attention and rumor, though. Her adoption into the Kingston family and recent pregnancy, on the other hand, would.

Janet was just behind them. She had taken too long choosing a dress for today and was running to catch up.

"It's my first day at this school, too," she reminded Lila as she caught her breath.

Lila smiled. It was true, Janet's first day in high school. She wrapped an arm around the younger girl's shoulders and then took her hand.

The first day went much better than Lila had hoped. A few boys leered at her and made comments about "easy pickings," and a few of the girls seemed to turn their noses up whenever she approached their desks or tables. Most people, however, didn't take much notice of her at all, beyond the novelty of her presence. Fort Garland wasn't so large that new people came to the community every day.

Several of her classes were with Marlene, which she appreciated. They'd be able to do homework and possibly occasional projects together.

All unease had evaporated by the end of day, when she met up with Janet. The young girl was surrounded by older boys and seemed to be crying. Lila stalked up and pushed her way into their circle. She didn't listen to what the boys were saying, just took Janet's shoulders and shook her gently.

"Are you all right?" Lila asked. "Did any of them hurt you?"

"Nah, we don't wanna hurt her," one of the boys jeered. "You going to stay for the fun, too, slut?"

Lila's eyes went cold. She held Janet in the crook of one arm and drew herself up. Her mother had taught her a few things, and poise was at the top of the list.

"Why don't you go, Janet? I'm sure Marlene is just over there." With a nudge, Lila started her younger sister walking away, taking her place at the center of the ring.

"Yeah, you're looking for someone new, aren't you? Now that baby's freed you up again."

Lila smirked a little. "You're right. I would like someone..." she hiked the skirt they were all eying to just above her knees, gripping it in fists, "to catch me," she finished, running with all her might for home. She spied Janet and Marlene as she passed them, the boys hot on her trail. None were nearly as fast as she.

The wind whistled in her ears. Her blood pounded and her breath came in long, full gulps. God, she loved to run. The boys' steps faded behind her. Glancing over her shoulder, she saw several of them clutching their chests, panting. Others simply slowed, not deeming her worth chasing.

She turned and laughed harder, catching back up to her sisters where they were walking.

"Boo!" she yelled behind them.

Janet screamed, but Marlene just laughed with Lila. Janet looked around for the boys, but they'd been left behind.

"How?"

Lila shrugged. "Don't let them bother you. No matter what they say about me, hold your head up." She demonstrated, drawing her back straight.

"You look tall!" Janet cried. Lila was normally taller than either of them, but her posture added to that. Janet imitated and looked at Marlene, who snickered.

"I don't think that works on sisters," she said, "but you do look taller anyway." Janet smiled and put the bounce back into her step. Lila did the same.

***

George sat behind Adam and Daphne. They were next to the district attorney behind the prosecutor's bench. The lawyer shuffled through his papers, muttering quietly to himself.

"How you holding up?" he asked the pair, looking from one to the other. Both were decidedly pale, almost ashen. They were dreading this. Neither answered, just looking to him with wide eyes.

The girls were at school, but Justin sat on Eva's lap next to him. George hugged his wife and kissed his grandson. The baby smiled up at him, showing several teeth now. He had just had his first birthday and was sampling solid food, beginning with the oatmeal cookie he held. He loved Daphne's cookies, gumming them up before finally breaking pieces from them.

Feeling eyes on him, George looked to his right. Across the aisle, Joshua Spencer stared openly. Eva noticed him as well, and shifted uncomfortably. Then the doors to the courtroom opened and a bailiff led in James and his lawyer. The defense came over and pulled the DA aside for a quiet exchange.

The DA came back to the newlyweds. "He's countering our plea bargain. He'll plead guilty to a single count of sexual assault of a minor and one of assault. It's not aggravated assault, Adam, just assault. The single count will still be on his record, keeping him from any position with minors, but the judge is unlikely to agree to very much jail time. Still, it would prevent the trial. You wouldn't have to testify or hear his account, either. It's up to you. I don't know that I can make our charges stick, but I'm pretty sure we have enough evidence." His voice trailed off, leaving the decision with the victims.

George looked at Eva, who shrugged. They didn't know anything about court cases or battles.

"Your fee?" Daphne whispered.

The lawyer shook his head, "Out of his fine. He'll have that regardless."

She looked at Adam and nodded. Adam ground his teeth. "If we don't take both, we still have to do this, don't we?" he asked.

The DA nodded, "Unless we have a counter offer."

Adam looked at Daphne. "I love you. All I want is you." Then he turned his face up to the lawyer. "Three counts of sexual assault." Daphne squeaked. "That's how many I saw, I want him to pay for each."

"What about Lila?" George asked quietly, not really wanting to interrupt. "Will she still be able to lay charges of her own?"

The DA met his eyes. "I haven't looked at her case. Certainly, this wouldn't preclude any unrelated charges." George settled back, waiting with his daughter and son-in-law.

"I'll counter. I'll be right back." The DA went to the defendant's bench, bending his head to talk to the other lawyer. Then he left the room.

Daphne's eyes went wide. "Where is he going?" she asked in a quiet, high-pitched whine.

"Shhh," Adam consoled her. "He said he'd be right back."

Justin seemed to sense his mother's panic and began fussing. Eva rocked him, but he was having none of it, flailing madly.

"Give him to me?" Daphne asked, reaching over the banister separating her from the row of seats. Justin stilled in her arms, taking the cookie she held out. Daphne brushed his hair flat and kissed his forehead. "There's my boy. Mama's good boy."

James was staring now, too. "That's not her baby," he said aloud. His lawyer cautioned him to stay quiet.

The DA came back in and smiled at the happy baby in Daphne's arms. "It's still hard thinking of you or Lila as a mother. They took the deal. I brought it to the judge, and he agreed to the sentencing I put on the table. So ... this should be over very soon."

Just then a loud voice called for everyone to rise. A white-haired man in a long black robe came in from the side and stepped up to the desk on the dais.

"James Spencer," he said dryly. "You are accused of three counts of sexual assault against a minor and one count of assault. How do you plead?"

His mouth distorted in hate and anger, but James only scowled at the judge until his lawyer answered, "We plead guilty, Your Honor."

"Then I hereby sentence you to seven years in jail, with three years to be served before you are eligible for parole. In addition, you will be fined five thousand dollars to be paid to the victims. Court is adjourned."

The sighs throughout the room were audible. Both sides of the room seemed relieved. Daphne hugged Justin who smiled and tugged at her hair. James fought the bailiff's grip on his elbow.

"Whose baby is that?" he asked harshly.

"Ours," Adam answered coldly, his hand on Daphne's shoulder, stroking her collarbone. She had turned from the aisle, into Adam, hiding her face.

James was hauled off then, his mother chasing after. They passed a woman rising on the aisle, thin, with spiky blonde hair. The DA had gone over to the other bench to shake hands with James' lawyer. Eva took Justin from Daphne, who started crying into Adam's chest. The baby was fussing again but accepted Eva's distraction of silly faces, laughing even.

Joshua moved more slowly, crossing the aisle. He stopped next to George, not approaching Daphne or Adam.

"I'm really sorry for what my son did to you and your family," he said carefully. "I know I didn't do enough to raise them proper, letting Nancy do far too much..." He shook his head. "Well, I can't fix it. I just hope you'll accept my apology." He held a hand out to George who took it.

"I imagine you, like me, had no idea what was going on at the time." George watched for Josh's reaction and wasn't disappointed. The man's blue eyes went wide and his mouth opened as his head shook.

"No! God, no, George, I would have stopped him! I would have told you at least, so you could protect your daughter. No." He growled. "Nancy knew. I'm sure of it. If I could ..." He closed his eyes and hung his head, looking beaten for all that his son was the offender, not the victim. He sighed heavily. "What James' said, about the baby, he's right, isn't he? Your new daughter carried him."

He looked around George to Justin in Eva's arms. He squinted a little and shook his head again. George grumbled but stepped aside a bit for him to see. Eva came forward as well, not eager, but not uneasy, either.

"Grandson?" Josh asked.

George's eyes narrowed. "Yes, mine," he growled.

Josh shook his head again. "Mine, too, I think. That's James' son, isn't it?"

George sighed. "Adam is his father," he reminded Joshua. "Legally, I mean. They adopted him from Lila. And since she is still a minor, I don't think James wants to be named his biological father, do you?

Joshua started. "I didn't mean ... I just ..." he sighed heavily. "I don't know what I mean. May I see him?"

Daphne reached out to her mother, stopping her. "Why?" she asked softly.

"Just to hold my grandson. I imagine it will be years before I have one legitimately." He shuffled his feet.

Daphne weighed him for a moment, then released her mother. "Just today."

He nodded, but smiled at all of them, taking Justin in his arms. The boy, cookie in hand again, looked up at the strange man, mouth open in an expression similar to Joshua's. The biggest difference was the curve at the corners of the man's open mouth.

George tried not to hold the deeds of son against the father, but he was relieved when Joshua handed Justin back to him.

"Thank you. Thank you so much." The first he said to George, the second to Daphne. Then he left the room as well.

***

Patty entered the courtroom wearing dark-tinted glasses. Once away from the windows of the hall, she plucked them off, blinking wearily. She wasn't hung-over, just awake earlier than usual. She didn't normally roll out of bed until eleven.

There was a quiet hum of whispers from the various people filling the benches. She recognized the Kingstons from Daphne's wedding. Her mother held James' son, currently destroying a cookie by drool alone. He was cute. He frightened her less today, only a baby.

She recognized James' father, too, Joshua. He sat a few rows ahead of her, just behind the table James and his lawyer would sit at.

Patty turned as the door creaked open. Daphne and Adam came in with their lawyer, looking nervous. By the charges listed, she was hardly surprised. Sexual assault was one thing James hadn't inflicted upon her. His physical and verbal abuse had been enough. She wasn't good enough to rape.

The bitterness of the thought continued to bubble in her as the woman she despised most in the world entered the courtroom. Nancy Spencer wore an impeccable navy blue dress suit. Her hair was perfectly curled around her face, turning the light touching it into a halo.

Patty smirked as she shifted, her leg snaking out into the aisle and tripping the imperious woman. It took control not to snicker as Nancy grabbed the back of a bench to catch herself. Those needle sharp blue eyes, the ones that had bore into her own years ago, shot spite again.

"You thought James liked you, girl? You were never more than a dalliance, a waste of all our time."

The door had closed on Nancy's tinkling laughter. That was when Patty had realized James was gone. Nancy would never have addressed Patty herself if James had been there. For that matter, the witch would probably have had her husband do it.

Patty liked Joshua, just as she had once liked James. He was rough and used the worst language imaginable, but the way he jumped at the sound of his wife's voice, the lash of her tongue, left little doubt that he obeyed Nancy as readily as Patty obeyed James.

Patty was not cowed by that piercing stare today. Today was for justice, as much for herself as for the couple on the other side of the railing. She met Nancy's cool eyes with her own icy glare. Her family would get what it deserved today.

Nancy flinched slightly, mouth twisting in disgust before moving to sit beside her husband. He shuffled a little away from his wife, a motion not lost on Patty. They had just stilled when James was brought in. Patty didn't try to trip him, but while everyone else shied from him, she stared openly.

He had changed. He was still large, still able to deal pain from those hands, but he was thinner, too. Dark circles had appeared under his eyes, hinting of rough nights. Unless Patty was mistaken, the red under the left was from a fist. He'd taken a little of his own behind bars.

His eyes met hers and he smiled, a predatory baring of teeth, an expression she knew and shrank from. He and the bailiff had passed before she remembered that he couldn't touch her now, held as he was. She shifted in her seat anxious for this to begin and end.

There was something going on between the lawyers, and the baby in Mrs. Kingston's arms began to fuss. The baby went to Daphne, who quieted him quickly. Odd. Where was the child's mother, the redhead?

James seemed confused, too. "That's not her baby!" he called from where he sat. Patty couldn't help but smile when his lawyer told him to shut the hell up. It wasn't long after the outburst that everyone was standing for the judge's entrance.

This was it. The man who had ruined her life was going to meet justice. Patty was surprised how quickly it came. There wasn't any testifying, no accounts, just charges and a guilty plea. The wind wasn't knocked from her sails for long. That gavel falling and James being pulled by cuffed hands was invigorating.

Nancy, distraught, followed her son and the bailiff. Patty resisted the urge to trip her this time. Instead, she walked sedately out behind them, amidst the other observers. Unnoticed and unremarked, she was free. She could do what she needed and move on.

***

Pushing herself from the floor, Patty lashed out. She was as skinny as ever, and her punch had little force behind it, but her boyfriend froze in disbelief.

After Neil, Patty had found a few other patrons, former classmates, ones that hadn't known her well, that had also wanted to "date" her. She had screwed up most of those, chasing the men off as quickly as Neil, but by the time Hugh had approached her, she had a better idea how she should respond. She hadn't counted on him being so much like James. It had started small, as it always did, wanting to know where she was, who she was with. She wasn't going to go through this again.

"Oh you are going to pay for that," he said, his voice malicious. It wasn't an unfamiliar tone to Patty.

"No," she said coldly. "You are." She was wearing her jacket, and her knife was in the pocket. He lunged for her and the knife came up, stabbing him in the chest.

His eyes went wide as he clutched the wound, holding the knife in him. "You fucking bitch. You think you're worth anything? You think you can stand up and I'll listen? You're just a strung out whore. I know how you used to get men, how you used to score your hits. I just thought this would be cheaper."

Flipping up the collar of the jacket nearly over her ears, she turned for the door. "You tell me how much cheaper it is, you pig." She lit up a cigarette on the doorstep. A habit she'd picked up from Hugh, she didn't regret it. Completely legal, the nicotine gave her that push she needed to move sometimes.

She was caught off-guard when a pair of officers were waiting for her outside the bar. "Patricia Wood, we need you to come with us."

"Uh, let me tell my boss." She opened the door and shouted. "Waylon, I'm going to the cop shop."

"What?!" he yelled back, but the door was swinging shut and she was walking away, a uniformed man on either arm.

"Let me guess," she muttered, not looking up at either man. "Hugh Newman."

"You know Hugh Newman?" one asked, but Patty didn't answer, following silently. She continued to sit silent when they threatened her, interrogated her, asking where she'd been the night before, if she had a knife. She wasn't smart, but she wasn't stupid either. She knew she needed a lawyer. When she finally got one, he flopped into the chair beside her, pulling out her list of previous offenses. None were heinous, indecent exposure, one other case of assault, disorderly conduct, nothing that warranted more than a night in the drunk tank and a fine. Come to think of it, she hadn't paid most of those ... that might be a problem.

"Why did you stab him, Patty?" the man in the rumpled suit asked.

She shrugged. "I didn't feel like being beaten anymore."

He shook his head. "I'm not sure I can make self-defense stick. Do you have any recent evidence of him beating you?"

She shook her head, snuffing out her filter. "Nope. He'd been out of town, given me a taste of freedom again. Reminded me I like it."

The lawyer chuckled sardonically. "I'll get a hold of his lawyer. We can probably cop a plea." He rose and left her staring at the empty table top, wondering where the freedom had gone. James was still in jail, wasn't he? He should have been, but she couldn't recall now. How many years was his sentence? She just remembered the happy feeling she'd had the day he was convicted, and now she was probably going to follow him into a cell. Fate was a real bitch.

Chapter Twenty-Two

George looked at the woman before him and felt his throat close. She turned in her white dress, taking the flowers he held out to her.

"Are you okay, Daddy?" she asked, her red hair curled around her cheeks.

He shook his head to clear the tears from his eyes. "Just ... not sure I'm ready to give away another daughter."

Lila laughed. "Well, it'll be the last time," she said lightly.

He huffed. "That doesn't make it better."

Hugging him, she still chuckled. "I'm sure it doesn't. I'll still be yours. You can't get rid of me now."

George laughed, hugging her back. "I never wanted to be rid of you, Lila."

"I know. That's what amazed me most of all." Tears thickened her voice, too. "That and finding a man I could love as much as you." The tears fell now; George felt them on his neck. "No boyfriend was ever as good to me, or anyone else, as you. Not until Aaron."

George patted her back, and Lila straightened. "Well, I guess we should get moving."

"Dad," Lila said, stopping him. "I've talked to Aaron, and ... I'm going to keep your name."

George's brow furrowed. "You're ..."

Lila nodded. "I know it's not common, but more and more ladies are keeping their maiden name. After all, all my students already know me as Ms. Kingston." She beamed at him.

"Well," he mused, taking her arm in his, "that takes some of the sting out."

She smiled broadly, kissing a bristled cheek. Daphne poked her head in. "Ready? Everyone else is."

Lila nodded and George led her down the aisle behind his eldest daughter. Little Shelly, Marlene's oldest at four, led the way, scattering petals.

"I love you, Daddy," Lila whispered as the march began.

"I love you, too, Lila."

***

Prison turned out to be even less of an ordeal than Patty expected. Sure, she'd pissed off a couple of top bitches, but she'd been able to steer clear of them for the most part. It had surprised her when she'd been offered courses, college courses. She had to pay for them, but they were cheaper than she expected. They also had a drug recovery program. She'd been off the hard stuff long enough that she didn't need it now, but she almost wished she'd gotten arrested for something serious sooner.

The part that really surprised her was when she was assigned a therapist.

"You want me to see a shrink?" she asked the warden, skeptically.

"Everyone gets a weekly session while they're here. You can sleep on his couch for all I care," the burly woman said rolling her eyes. "I think that's what most of them do."

Patty shrugged and followed the woman. It wasn't as though she had a choice, not for a few more months. Thankfully, her sentence was brief. She'd only get one term of classes in, but that might be enough to get her the high school diploma she never finished. Why not, while she was being housed and fed?

The guard opened the door to a small room, not far from the visiting area. She wasn't surprised she'd never gotten visitors, except Waylon once. To Patty's surprise, there was a couch and a chair. The room was undecorated, concrete walls making the furniture look even more out of place.

Still, it had been a long time since she'd had a comfortable seat anywhere, and she moved to the couch quickly, taking little notice of the round woman in the chair. Once she was seated, feet on one arm of the sofa, head on the other, she smirked. "What's up, doc?" She'd seen the Loony Tunes in the cinema, a lifetime ago.

"Please put your feet down," the woman said with a small sigh. "Would you like tea?" she asked.

Patty ignored the request. The chunky woman wore blue with a bright red scarf tied around her head. "Nah, thanks," she muttered. Seeing the woman's frown for her feet, Patty sighed loudly and sat up.

"What's up, Patty, is that you and I have very little time together, unless you choose to see me after your release. I'd like to make the most of the time we have." She sipped her tea before placing the china cup on a saucer. The woman had to have brought that and the teapot. Neither were from here.

"Who are you?" she asked, sure this wasn't just any shrink.

"My name is Wanda Peterson, Patty. I'm here to help you as much as I can in the time we have."